Praise for Liz Rosenberg

Home Repair

"Surprising moments of grace. . . . An absorbing tale where random acts of kindness abound. In the tradition of Jane Austen . . . Rosenberg's *Home Repair* is a keeper."

—*The Boston Globe*

"Rosenberg's prose sings in this winning novel with a fragile heroine capable of change and a cast of unique characters."

—Bette-Lee Fox, *Library Journal*, Starred Review

"A beautifully written tale of family and forging on."

—Malena Lott, Athena's Bookshelf

The Laws of Gravity

"A heart wrenching and honest exploration of family love and betrayal. A real page turner right up to its beautiful last page."

—Ann Hood, author of *The Red Thread* and *The Knitting Club*

"Drop whatever book you're reading and pick up a copy of Liz Rosenberg's stunning look at three Long Island families, *The Laws of Gravity*, told in clear-eyed, more often than not very funny prose . . . a family function/dysfunction novel melded with a legal thriller that would do justice to Scott Turow at his peak."

—*Huntington News*

"The best book written by a woman in the last twenty years."

—*Hakesher*

"Powerful and at the same time intensely delicate in its portrayal of the intimacies and contradictions in family life."

—David Park, author of *The Truth Commissioner*

The Moonlight Palace

"This sweet coming-of-age story weaves the blush of first love amid the dangers of political intrigue. Rich with historical detail and rounded out by an entertaining cast of characters, it is sure to enthrall historical fiction fans."

—Cortney Ophoff, *Booklist*

"Fascinating and unique. . . . Aggie's adventures in work, family, and love make for an inviting story that you will want to see through to the end."

—*San Francisco Book Review*

"This is a story filled with marvelous, and marvelously eccentric, characters. Not just the crumbling palace, but also Agnes's multi-generational family, built with both family of blood and family of choice into a slightly crazy whole. . . . Her world makes a terrific story."

—*Reading Reality*

"*The Moonlight Palace* is a wonderful novel, and it will draw you in, and keep you there, until it finally releases you."

—*Bibliotica*

Beauty and Attention

OTHER TITLES BY LIZ ROSENBERG

Demon Love

Home Repair

The Laws of Gravity

The Moonlight Palace

Beauty and Attention

A Novel

LIZ ROSENBERG

This is a work of fiction. Names, characters, organizations, places, events, and incidents are either products of the author's imagination or are used fictitiously.

Published by Lake Union Publishing, Seattle

www.apub.com

ISBN-13: 9781503940635
ISBN-10: 1503940632

Cover design by Laura Klynstra

Printed in the United States of America

To my daughter, Lily, the most beautiful and wonderful young woman I know

Chapter One

Libby Archer and her best friend, Henrietta, had put in a full day's work by noon. They'd started at dawn—folding, selecting, discarding items, dragging corrugated boxes across the floors of a house still in mourning, its shades drawn. The brick edifice, built a century earlier, clung to the cool of the previous evening. By midafternoon the heat would be stifling, no matter how Libby and the maid, Trilby, raced around opening and closing windows. Summer came sometimes early to Rochester, New York, and sometimes not at all. This had been a very hot June.

The two friends wore Bermuda shorts and wrinkled white blouses as they wandered about in their bare feet. Their toenails were painted a bright pinkish-red, Revlon's bestselling shade for 1954, Fire & Ice. Libby, the slighter of the two, wore her hair tied loosely back in a black band. The tall girl, Henrietta—Henry, as she was generally known—was gawky, with a long, bony face and clear green eyes. She sported a paisley bandanna, which hid her frizzy hair. Around her neck she'd hung a few impossibly long strands of colored glass beads.

Henry sank back on her heels with a sigh, surveying their morning's work. She blew a strand of hair out of her eyes. "We're getting there," she said. Most of the rooms, including this once-cluttered study, held nothing but boxes and furniture swathed in sheets.

Libby studied a photograph cradled in both hands. The man in the photo was her late father. She resembled him in the dark curves of her hair, the slimness of her figure, her susceptibility to passionate extremes of mood, her impatience, and her nearsightedness. In the photo he was grinning sardonically, looking away from the camera's eye, holding up a large fish. "He never went fishing after my mother passed away," said Libby. "I don't know why. You can see he loved it."

"I imagine he gave up a lot of things after your mother was gone," Henrietta said. "That is," she added, flustered, checking her friend's face for signs of a reaction, "one does."

"He did." Libby looked positively stricken for a moment. Then she smiled at the photograph, much as she might have smiled at her father when he was alive. A sad smile with equal parts affection and distance. She wiped the photo with a white cloth, removing dust from the glass. "I wish he'd given up other things instead. I miss him."

"I miss him too," Henry agreed. She had liked Mr. Archer, despite his faults. In her opinion, there had been many serious flaws. They had made Libby's life hard. Libby had sacrificed a great deal for him. She had given up any idea of a career—all of her many intense and enthusiastic ideas. She'd even turned down her scholarship to an eastern women's college to see Mr. Archer through his final stages of disintegration. Henry could not be as forgiving as her friend. But Mr. Archer had liked her—which was rare among her friends' parents.

Henrietta Capone was regarded as not just eccentric for a girl but downright dangerous. Her name, for instance, was a gangster's name. A decent young woman would have been married by now and rid herself of it. She was too tall, yet she wore heels, and she dressed like a gypsy, in flounced skirts and costume jewelry.

Libby kept studying her father's picture, as if she might find in it the clue to his absence. There was great sweetness of expression in her face.

That was Libby's real attraction, Henrietta thought—the unexpected way her smile animated her face, moving it from severity to something as open as a flower. And in how she appeared to be loosely floating when she walked, at ease in her shapely body. But it was generally believed, almost universally agreed, that Libby was *not* the beauty of her family. That honor went to Libby's fair-haired cousin Veronica, named "dazzling" by the Rochester *Times-Union* at the Grand Cotillion of 1946. Veronica was honey blonde, composed, and even-featured and could easily have been a model like Nena von Schlebrügge if she had wished it. Ninety-nine people out of a hundred would declare that Veronica had snagged "the looks" of the Archer girls, but that one person would disagree, and disagree violently, amazed by the stupidity of the rest. Mr. Lockwood was one of these rarities, Henrietta thought with satisfaction. But her satisfaction was short-lived.

"Does he even know you're leaving?" she asked Libby. She didn't need to identify the "he." She saw that by the slight wince on her friend's face.

"Everyone received the same note," Libby said quickly.

"He won't like it," Henrietta said.

"Fortunately," said Libby, with an impatient toss of her head, "I am not in a position to care what your friend Caspar Lockwood will like."

The two friends gazed at each other a moment. Henrietta decided not to press, this once. Instead she said, "*I* don't like it . . . Ireland is too far away."

A shadow fell across Libby's face. "It's not so far, Henry. One transatlantic flight. Hop across the pond."

"You'd better not start calling it *the pond*," warned Henry. "Or take up tea and scones, or come back talking with a fake Irish accent, saying *amongst* and *whilst*."

"But I do like tea." Libby grinned. "Whilst eating scones amongst the cream."

"No foxhunts, no tweeds," Henry went on relentlessly. "No marrying a Trinity man. None of that foreign baloney." She pushed the cuff of her white blouse up her arm, revealing a large, round, mannish-looking watch. "Speaking of tea . . . we have company again this afternoon, don't we?"

Libby hit her forehead and groaned.

Henrietta reached out one long arm and helped her friend to her feet. "Shame on you. It's your last for a long while. And you know they mean well."

"That's the worst of it, isn't it?" asked Libby with a wan smile.

Four hours later, washed, polished, and brushed, the same two young women sat side by side in the second parlor, almost unrecognizable from their disheveled morning selves. They would have passed muster in any ladies' magazine of the day. Henrietta had changed into a skirt and blouse, and Libby wore a plain black A-line dress, with black ballet-style slippers. Her thick, unruly brown hair was washed and brushed and rolled brilliantly over her shoulders, like a girl in the Breck shampoo ads. Henrietta's green skirt hung an inch too short, a fact she kept trying to hide by tugging the hem down over her knees. She did not succeed, and every minute or two the skirt popped up again, as short as before.

The parlor, once known as the Blue Room, had earned its name from its fading, china-blue wallpaper pattern. It was, in the final hours of Libby's residence in her father's house, the last room still fully furnished, making the rest of the house feel even emptier.

Guests who came to comfort the young mourner threaded their way through hot, bare halls and stacked boxes and shrouded furniture to reach the one remaining haven of upholstered chairs, shabby sofas, pictures, silk flowers in figured vases. The items in the room seemed to have merely accumulated without beauty or attention. Mr. Archer had been a man who refused to throw anything away. It could have been a room neglected from an earlier century; there was nothing up-to-date or 1950s about any of it. The residents appeared to have given up any effort to live in their own time, and simply squatted among the artifacts of the past.

"I don't understand," repeated their youngest visitor, Bridget Block, a pretty, plump blonde of sixteen who had not yet "come out." She sat close to her mother, a worthy matriarch of Rochester society. "Why are you visiting people in Ireland?"

"They are not people," Mrs. Block corrected her. "They are *family*." Like Libby, she wore black, though the June afternoon waxed sultry. Mrs. Block's looks had been sometimes compared to Doris Day's, a suggestion that thrilled her. She wore her hair in a Doris Day bob, but her chin had settled. She had been widowed ten years earlier by a man of industry. She knew that wearing black was the correct thing to do, especially on occasions like this, and she looked approvingly on Libby Archer, who had always been a dutiful and faithful daughter.

"Family is everything," intoned their eldest visitor, the Block grandmother, a sallow cricket of a woman. "What relation are these Irish people to you, dear, exactly?"

"My uncle and my cousin Lazarus," answered Libby. "My mother's family. We were very close when I was young." The old woman looked at her blankly. "My mother's people," Libby said a bit louder.

"You have relatives in *Ireland*?" insisted Bridget. "But that's in—in Europe—isn't it?"

Henrietta chuckled. The mother glared at her.

"I'm sorry," Henrietta said. "I thought she was joking."

"It is no joke to cross the ocean," said the grandmother. "In my day, of course, we had to travel by ship. But then, one will do anything for the sake of family."

"That's true, Mother," said Mrs. Block irritably. "And how many weeks will you be gone?" she asked Libby. "This has been so awful for you. Your poor father's decline . . ."

"The loss of a parent is a terrible thing," said the old woman. "The cruelest blow." She made a bubbling noise with her straw. Being mildly deaf, the old woman could not hear it and went on sucking till her daughter took the glass out of her hand.

"More iced tea?" Libby offered. "Bridget, would you like a cookie?"

"No thank you," her mother answered for the girl, who had leaned forward hopefully, her hand outstretched. "Bridget is watching her waist."

"I'll be gone a year or two," said Libby.

All the visitors' heads snapped toward her in surprise.

"Two *years*!" Bridget exclaimed. "Why in the world would you visit with family for *two years*?" Both her mother and grandmother shot her a warning glance, but they all regarded Libby with a mixture of curiosity and alarm.

"We had hoped," said Mrs. Block, "that you'd be settling down here in Rochester, and getting married."

"I have no plans," answered their young hostess, "to be married."

"Why, Libby! I had no idea you were the driven career-woman type," said Mrs. Block.

"Are those the only two possibilities?" Libby asked, pleasantly enough. A closer listener would have heard the steeliness in her voice.

"We thought that tall, good-looking man who's always hanging around—" Bridget began.

"Shh!" said her mother. "Men are unreliable. They change their minds. They die."

"Oh, men are beastly," Bridget agreed happily.

"I want to see the world," Libby said. She leaned closer, hands clasped together in a gesture of appeal, as if to convince her guests. "I thought it might comfort me."

"The world is not necessarily a comforting place," said the old woman, curving her veiny hand over Libby's and patting it. "But I wish you luck. Indeed I do."

"I don't see why you want to go to Europe," Bridget insisted. "It's so close to Russia. That's dangerous, isn't it, Mama? With the bomb and Communists and all. And there's so much going on right here in Rochester."

The doorbell chimed just then, and the maid, Trilby, entered, ushering in more visitors. This larger group threatened to overwhelm the room, so chairs were drawn from some mysterious supply, and seating rearranged. Henrietta jumped to her feet, glad to be in motion. But the new guests brought no relief.

"You poor orphaned darling!" cried one of the newcomers, her arms outstretched to Libby, who shrank back visibly. "All alone in the world!"

At the same moment another female visitor headed into the parlor. She aimed straight for Henrietta, as if she had been directed there. The stranger grasped Henry's arm with surprising strength.

"Is it true," she asked in a low voice, shaking Henry's arm, "that Libby Archer is getting married and selling this house?"

"No," gasped Henrietta.

"None of it?"

"I beg your pardon," said Henrietta, tugging her arm free. She kept her eye on her friend, hemmed in on all sides, her face thin and wan, like an orchid jutting from a jet black vase.

A man had just approached Libby and was saying in a loud voice, "Well, you've earned a jolly nice vacation, I'd say! What'll it be? Miami? Maine?"

"Is any of it true?" persisted the stranger. "Is she selling this house?"

"Not that I'm aware." Henrietta managed to pull her arm free, but the visitor was relentless.

The woman turned her head in all directions, birdlike. "My son has been looking for something in this neighborhood, and this house would do very well. He's just recently married, and his wife is very particular."

"I am . . . surprised to hear it," said Henrietta drily.

"How many bedrooms are there?" the woman went on. "At least six or seven, I'll bet."

"I haven't counted," said Henrietta.

"What on earth will you do with yourself now?" a young woman across the room asked Libby. Her friend had, Henrietta thought, the look of a wild animal caught in a cage. "Will you join some clubs? Will you go to *college*?"

"She's thinking of becoming a career woman," said Bridget.

"Ohhhh!" called out several voices at once.

"What's that now?" said the old woman.

"A *career*, Mother! Like a secretary. Or—or a nurse, I suppose."

"In my day," said the old lady, "only women who were jilted took on a career."

"I'm a career woman!" Henrietta announced suddenly. Her voice rang out more loudly than she had planned. Without meaning to, she was now addressing the entire room. Though she had an air of authority, she hated speaking in public more than anything in the world. Henry's voice shook with shy, nervous humor. At any instant she thought she might burst into hysterical laughter.

"Yes, I'm a journalist," she chattered on. "I write for magazines. Not anything as big as *LIFE*, but, well, I'm working on it. . . . Also newspapers. Small, regional papers mostly. Feature newspaper articles about people's lives. I am extremely interested in people." The guests went on gaping at her as if she had three heads. Libby shot her friend a grateful look, a wry smile twisting up her lips, and made her escape from the room.

❧

It was dusk, the sky a dusty-plum color, by the time all the comforters finally departed. Libby stood with her back to the door, her arms outstretched, as if to prevent the crowd from pushing its way back in while Trilby gathered up glasses of amber-colored ice tea and melting ice, shaking her head over spills and damp rings. Henry collapsed as soon as the final guest left, her legs dangling over the edge of a sofa.

Libby held her pose at the door a moment longer. "Well, *that* was fun," she said.

Henry did not answer. The silence of the brick house came as a relief. Together, wordlessly, the two moved to the square back porch, cooled by the shade of a red-leafed copper beech tree in the yard. Because they had been friends since grade school, they had spent countless hours together, and now the weight of those lost hours seemed to sink down on them all at once. They sat side by side on a glider, using the toes of their shoes to push themselves back and forth. The glider creaked. The beech tree's leaves sparkled like pennies.

"Tell me," Henry said. "How well do you know this Irish uncle and cousin?"

"There's an aunt too," Libby explained. "But she comes and goes."

"*That* must be nice," mused Henrietta.

"We knew them well when I was small," Libby went on. "Then there was a falling out with my father, after my mother died."

"I see," said Henrietta. Mr. Archer had fallen out with nearly everyone, sooner or later. Alcohol was usually at the center of it.

Libby went on. "They are as American as we are, only they have lived close to Belfast for many years now, on the Ards Peninsula. It's beautiful—I've seen pictures. Uncle Sachs is my mother's brother. Cousin Lazarus is five years older than I am—an only child. He was adopted. People always said he'd been gotten on the black market. There's something wrong with his heart, I think. He was a wonderful athlete as a boy, the fastest runner I ever saw. He was quite a character. When we were small, he kept plunking down on one knee to propose marriage."

"Then he had good taste," Henry said with a smile.

Libby stared at her black ballet flats. She flexed and pointed her feet at the end of her long, slim legs. "It's sad. He never married, or worked or really did anything," she said. "He never even got to finish school, because of poor health, and he was brilliant. He had beautiful, strange white-gold hair as a boy—towheaded, they called it. It made him look old. I'm sure it's darkened by now. They invited me the instant they heard about Father. My aunt will meet me in Dublin and take me up to the country house. Cousin Lazarus may be in a wheelchair by now."

"Well, don't let them introduce you to any unmarried Irish lords," Henrietta said. "We want you back exactly as you are. No changes."

Libby turned her clear gaze to her friend. "Why would I go into the world, just to oppose it? No." She shook her head slowly but firmly. "I haven't seen anything. I haven't done anything! Please don't tell me not to change. I hope to be completely transformed."

"Then I'd better visit before you become unrecognizable," Henrietta said.

Libby reached for Henry's empty glass. "I wish you would! People say they'll do things, and then don't follow through."

Henry hung on to the glass an instant, forcing Libby to look at her. "I always do as I promise. So does Mr. Lockwood. He may be pigheaded and stubborn, but I've never known him to go back on his word. Have you?"

"Were we talking about Cap Lockwood?" asked Libby.

"I was hoping to be."

"I wish you wouldn't," said Libby. She left to get more lemonade, but on her way out she gave her friend's swing a vigorous push from behind.

Henry shut her eyes and swayed back and forth in the sun. "He'll need a helping hand, that man . . ."

Chapter Two

The office of Lockwood Inc. ran according to a logical and well-considered system. The rooms had a stripped-down, functional look—the furniture was all Danish Modern, in light wood and curved, clean lines. Caspar Lockwood, the company's energetic young founder, president, and proprietor, typically wore a white shirt, dark jacket, and narrow tie. His male employees, taking no chances, followed suit.

It was with a grim and focused air that two men bent over the same desk, on which sat a square black phonograph.

"Let's hear the worst," said Lockwood.

The other man made a slight motion. There was an audible scratching sound, a steady clicking, and then a man's voice began to wail:

> My baby took the sugar,
> I'm feeling blue.
> She lef' me high and dry,
> What can I do?
> My baby lef' me, lef' me, lef' me . . .

The needle stuck, the other man hurried to lift it while Caspar Lockwood groaned, striking his forehead with the heel of his hand.

"I'm very sorry, sir," said the younger man.

"What if we calibrate the needle?" Lockwood asked.

"You mean *re*calibrate it, sir."

Lockwood made a tent of his hands and covered his nose and mouth with it, peering at the other man. He spoke through his hands. "We've already done it?"

"Three times."

Lockwood tapped his fingertips together. Then he leaned forward onto the desk again. "What are we doing wrong?"

"I'm sorry," said the other.

"I'm not accusing you. I am asking: what are we getting wrong? It's not the needle, obviously."

"I don't think so, sir. We have the best needle on the market."

Lockwood nodded. "Good. What then? Don't be afraid to say."

"Perhaps—" the man hesitated. "Perhaps the material of the playing disk, the record itself. There may be a way to refine the grooves, to extend playing time."

"Interesting. So, something like . . ."

"Metals might work. At faster and at slower speeds. For instance, lightweight aluminum. I was thinking—"

There was a knock on the door, and a younger man entered, dressed like the other two but with a more rumpled appearance.

"Cousin Caspar," the young man said. "Someone's here to see you."

"Who is it?" barked the man. "What do they want?"

"It's a person named Libby Archer—"

Lockwood made a gesture of surprise that sent a jar of pencils flying.

"Never mind," he said, his voice sounding suddenly younger, lighter, and if possible, even more energetic. "Let it be. Let it. Send her in, Richie."

Libby Archer, dressed in her slim black sheath, appeared in the doorway. "I've sent myself in." Her smile looked uncertain.

Lockwood scrambled to his feet. He was long-legged, muscular, and looked at that moment a little menacing. "Ah. All right. Roger, we'll talk again later. Thank you. Thanks very much."

The other two men scattered as if they'd been shot at.

"Libby," Caspar said, pointing with one broad hand. "Have a seat. Please."

She sat. People tended to obey Lockwood without thinking. He waited till she was seated to resume his own chair. He placed two pencils side by side on his desk and nudged them together. His expression was more reserved than welcoming. "You are coming to see me in my place of business," he said. "That can't mean anything good."

"I am going away soon," Libby said. "To Ireland. Henrietta thought I ought to tell you in person."

Instead of answering, the firm-looking young man rummaged for something in his top desk drawer and removed a small printed card. He had a stern, dark appearance, and often seemed to be scowling when he wasn't. He tossed the card faceup on the desk between them. "Yes," he said. "I received this announcement. I guess all your nearest and dearest friends got them."

"I'm sorry," said Libby, "if it seemed impersonal."

"It has your address in Ireland," he said, waving a hand. "A phone number. But it doesn't say how long you will be gone. Or when you'll be back. Or more importantly, why you are going."

"We don't always know why we do things."

Cap looked at her steadily, his brown eyes so dark they appeared nearly black. Libby had often heard the phrase *a burning gaze*, but she had never personally experienced one. She might be turned to cinders if she held still another instant. She looked away, feeling the heat rush away from her face.

"I expect to be gone at least a year," she said.

"A year!" said Lockwood, registering surprise. "I don't like it. I don't approve."

Libby made a sudden motion—of rebellion—as if his words had betrayed him. "*You* don't approve," she echoed, "of my having some freedom."

"Don't pretend to misunderstand me," he said. "I don't mean approval in the conventional sense. You and I are not conventional. But I don't approve of this plan. It's a bad one."

"I didn't know that I needed your approval even of a bad plan," said Libby, struggling to keep her voice under control.

"I hope you'd want it, though."

She appeared to study the desk. "I'll always be glad of your good opinion," she said.

"You asked me to wait," he said.

"I asked nothing of the kind!" she exclaimed, both hands flat on the desk. "I said nothing was possible so long as my father was ill."

"He is ill no more," said Lockwood. Libby's head jerked up at this, but his expression had remained gentle. "How much time do you want now?" His voice was husky and soft.

"As much as I need."

"A year? Two years?"

"Let us say two," Libby answered with a smile.

"You say that too easily," he snapped. "Why not ten years?"

Libby's mouth hardened. "Let's say ten then. A decade will be better. Come see me in ten years."

"Where, exactly? Here, in my office? Or—" He leaned forward, as if to spring across the desk. He read from the printed card. "At Strangford, the Ards Peninsula, County Down. Tell me the time and place, Libby, and I will set my watch and my compass by them."

"Don't raise your voice," said Libby.

He ignored this. "In ten years, in twenty, I will be the same. I am not changeable. The instant I saw you I was no longer master of my own soul. No. To be truthful, your looks didn't captivate my attention at first. It was the sound of you. Maybe the smell of you too, if I'm being honest. But once I heard you speak, I'd never have settled for anyone else."

She tried to speak lightly. "What momentous thing did I say?" She crossed her legs and jiggled her foot impatiently.

"You said, 'I would like to take this book out of the library.' And you set it down in front of me with a thud. Your jaw was clenched, just as it is now. The book was *War and Peace*." He laughed, a short bark. "An ambitious choice. And did you ever read it, Libby? Did you finish it?"

She said nothing.

"Did you get even, let's say, halfway through? You're blushing, so I guess not. You have a good mind, Libby, but it doesn't settle. You busy yourself with one distraction after another. You flit from one thought, one burning cause, one impulse to the next. You need to take hold of something. Why not take hold of me?" He held one strong, square, tanned hand out, appealingly. She looked at it a long moment before she answered.

"I think I must take hold of myself before I reach for anyone else."

"That's too easy. It's unworthy of you."

Her temper gave way. "Should I go straight from my father's house to a husband's? To be a model housewife, sitting in a new split-level with an electric clothes dryer and brand-new automatic coffeemaker? Is that the fate you consider worthy?"

He laughed bitterly. "You think I want to enslave you. It is to set you free that I wish to marry you—to make you as free as possible in your body and soul."

"Oh yes," said Libby, with a sardonic smile. "I understand your desire well enough."

"I don't think you do." He rolled his shoulders impatiently. At that instant, he looked like the champion amateur boxer he had been a decade earlier. "I doubt you understand your own desires, much less mine. Do you think it's easy to move through the world as a single young woman, even in 1954? I'm afraid you'll find it a tight fit. And," he added, "you will marry someone else."

"Whatever else you fear, don't be afraid of that."

His mouth tightened. "So you say." He bit the words off. "You've said other things to me as well—things you did not mean."

"Are you accusing me of leading you on?" Her color was suffused, and her eyes sparkled with threatening tears, bringing out the orange fire in the iris.

"Do you deny it?"

Both were breathing hard. Libby turned away first. "I am sorry that you love me. I didn't ask for it. I don't see why I am to blame for it."

"Don't you?" He leaned toward her.

"No," she said simply. "And sometimes I think you hate me. You're always angry at me."

He shook his head. His hair, while dark, was fine. His skin was coppery. He was sometimes mistaken for an American Indian, with his black straight hair and dark, even features. "Not angry, Libby. Disappointed."

"Believe me, I have no interest at this moment in disappointing—or marrying—anyone."

"That's cold comfort. You're running away, Libby. Call it what you like. Fear is dangerous. You will find someone. Or they will find you. And it will be the wrong person. "

"Have you turned to fortune-telling now?" She leaned across the desk and touched his arm. "Cap, I wish we could be friends."

He glanced at her hand on his arm. "I have enough friends. I don't need more."

She seemed stricken, though she tried to cover it by speaking evenly. "I'm sorry to hear it. I think one can never have too many friends." She attempted a laugh, which failed. She stood and nervously smoothed down her black dress. "I'm very sorry if I seem to have changed my mind. Truly. Of course, it's a woman's prerogative—"

"If you're going to use stupid clichés, you may as well get out."

"That is unkind," she said steadily. "My father just died. I am trying to find my way."

"You're right, you are right," he muttered, almost to himself. He clutched at his head. "Then why don't I believe you?"

"You think I'm lying? That my plan is to go to Ireland and marry someone else?"

"No," he groaned. "I don't think you're lying to me—you're lying to yourself!" His face was very dark at that moment, suffused with passion and, if Libby had admitted it to herself, very handsome. "You're playing dumb. Telling yourself nonsense about what Libby Archer wants and needs. Travel abroad. Independence. You repeat these stories to yourself like a child with a favorite fairy tale. But it's a hand-me-down story, not your own."

"You accuse me of never finishing my books." She twisted a small gold ring around and around on her pinky finger. It had belonged to her mother, a long time ago.

"Well, you'll finish this one whether you like it or not."

"You always think the worst of me!" she burst out. "You charge me with teasing, with flirting, deliberately lying. You tell me I am full of clichés; I am inauthentic. Why would you wish to be with such a person?"

"There's no accounting for taste," he said.

"I am not joking!" she said, near tears.

"Neither am I."

"You seem to enjoy tormenting me."

His voice was steely. But every movement he made, even the slightest motion of his fingers, expressed longing. Had he been a cat, he would have sprung into her lap. "Do I seem to be enjoying myself now?"

"Oh, I told myself I wouldn't cry!" she said, bursting into passionate tears. "No, stay away!" she warned, as he stood and approached. She put up her hands, as if she felt herself to be really in danger. "Don't come any closer."

He wheeled around. "You are a damnable creature! I will leave you here to compose yourself." He headed to the office door.

"Just go!" she shouted after him vehemently. "I'll be long gone before you get back."

Chapter Three

Under certain circumstances, Lazarus Sachs thought, quoting, or more likely misquoting, something he'd once read: Under certain circumstances, there are few hours in life more agreeable than the hour dedicated to the ceremony known as afternoon tea.

The expanse of lawn behind Gardencourt, their fine, old Irish country house, was as velvety green as a billiard table. It overlooked the softly swelling drumlins and gorse hedgerows in the middle distance, but served almost as an extension of the house itself. The lawn was currently laid out for an elaborate tea, with white wicker chairs, a low table, and a scattering of books, gadgets, musical instruments, and oriental rugs.

Old Mr. Sachs sat in the deepest of the chairs, a bright-colored pillow at his back and an ancient paisley shawl over his legs. A border collie lay curled at his feet. The dog's bright-amber eyes never left his owner's face. Mr. Sachs held aloft a large persimmon-colored teacup in his hand, his eyes shut, as if drinking the last remaining sun of the June day. Daytime had done what it could; shadows lay long and flickering against the green turf. One could smell, if not quite see from here, the salty Irish coastline nearby. The sun would not reach its zenith for a few more hours, but the cool of evening came swirling in.

Lazarus and another young man, firm and fine of figure, strolled behind the old man's chair, engaged in quiet, lively conversation. A smaller mutt dog romped at their feet, nearly tripping them up several times. Had Mr. Sachs turned to observe the young men, he would have noticed a striking contrast, for Lord Warburton was tall, fair-haired, and muscular, the very picture of health, while his only son, Lazarus, was all too obviously a walking invalid.

Lord Warburton's nose might be a shade too large; one gray-blue eye, if one looked closely, appeared to gaze slightly to one side, as if in deference to the speaker—his features were neither small nor even. One might have said that his thin upper lip was too stiff—whether from a lack of sensuality or an excess of it, no casual observer could have guessed. Yet the overall appearance was unquestionably good; people liked and trusted Warburton on sight.

Lazarus, on the other hand, portrayed illness and lack of grace with every move. His clothing was ill fitting and out of date, as if he'd long ago given up looking in a mirror; he wore the sort of dandyish velvet smoking jacket that might have been popular in the 1930s. Lazarus did not walk so much as shamble, and his hands habitually strayed nervously into his pockets. His face was lean, homely, and wolfish, with a yellowish cast. His hair, a striking pale shade of whitest gold, made him appear both older and more childish than his twenty-six years. Each time he walked past his father, he gazed at him with love and a tenderness he disguised with ceaseless antics and teasing—placing a napkin on his father's head as he walked by and then removing it the next time he passed, handing him a fan of leaves, or ruffling the old man's thinning white hair.

Whatever Lazarus was saying—and he talked nearly nonstop—it made his companion chuckle, with murmurs of disapproval: "I say, you don't really mean that," and, "Even you don't believe what you are saying."

"What are you going on about?" asked the father at last.

"Absolute nonsense!" declared Lord Warburton. "Lazarus says the world will be ruled by machines. He claims we will let them think and talk and calculate for us . . . even trust them to find our wives. He says we'll find our immortality hidden in the entrails of some mechanical device."

The son came round in front of his father's chair, and made a minute adjustment in relation to the angle of the sunlight. At any moment it might rain. At any moment anywhere in Ireland, it could rain, always. Lazarus stooped before the old man, and in the instant their steady gazes locked, one saw at last the real bond between father and son.

"Stop fussing. I'm getting on quite well," said the father.

"Have you drunk your tea?"

The father lifted his empty cup. "Yes, and enjoyed it."

"Can I get you some more?"

The old man considered it. "Well, maybe. I'll wait and see," he said. "Don't want to rush into anything." His way of speaking, even after decades of living in his adopted country, was plainly American.

"Are you cold?" asked Lazarus. "There's a breeze blowing."

The father rubbed his legs experimentally. "Can't tell unless I feel."

"Shall I fetch someone to feel for you?" asked his son, teasingly.

"Oh, someone will always feel for me. That's the luxury of being old. Don't *you* feel for me, Lord Warburton?"

"Of course." The larger man, who had been playing with the small dog, answered immediately. His clipped accent marked him as an Englishman. There was none of the soft burr and lilt of the North Irish. "Though you do look wonderfully comfortable, I must say."

"I reckon I am, mostly." The old man smoothed the wool shawl over his knees. "The truth is we've been comfortable so many years I just don't notice anymore."

"Yes, that's the bore of comfort," said Lord Warburton. "I would think you'd be miserable under that heavy wool shawl, though."

"No, he must have the shawl!" cried the son. "Don't put ideas into his head."

"It's my wife's shawl," said the old man, simply. "I'll have to give it back to her when she comes."

"You'll do nothing of the sort," objected his son. "You'll keep it to cover your poor old legs."

"Hey," objected the old man. "I guess my legs are as good as yours."

"That's not saying much, Daddy. I'm a poor specimen." Lazarus shook out one skinny leg woefully. "Won't you have more tea? This comes from Paris." Lazarus lifted the lid of the teapot and sniffed at it. "I can't tell it from Lipton's," he admitted.

"'Valor is stability, not of legs and arms, but of courage and the soul.' Montaigne." The father held up the cup, while the son poured. "My boy is an excellent sick-nurse, Lord Warburton. I call him my sick-nurse because he's such a sick boy himself."

"Daddy!" the ugly young man exclaimed.

"Well, you are. I wish you weren't. But I guess you can't help it, after all."

"Montaigne suffered all his life from kidney stones," said Lazarus, setting the tea back on the table and stuffing his hands back into the pockets of his shabby black velvet jacket.

Lord Warburton let out a low whistle of admiration, looking from father to son.

"We are a fount of useless information," Lazarus admitted.

"Were you ever sick, Lord Warburton?" the father asked.

Lord Warburton considered it. "Yes, sir, once, in the Persian Gulf."

"He's making light of you, Daddy," said Lazarus. "Warburton is a great tease." He fiddled with a radio lying on the grass, till some jazz music came on with a spurt of saxophones. "Ah! Hear that?" He listened with a hungry, rapt expression.

The old man grimaced. "That sounds like machine-gun fire, not music. I don't understand any of the new tastes—not the new humor, not the songs. It's a sure sign of old age. But you don't look like you've been ill a day in your life, Lord Warburton."

"Warburton's sick of life, he says. He was just telling me so; going on and on about it," said Lazarus.

"Is that so?" asked the old man seriously.

"Your son is the wrong man to come to. Doesn't believe in anything at all—nothing but music and machines."

"It's because of his illness," explained the father. "Lazarus feels he never had a chance. But he's really the most buoyant human being I've ever known. Like one of those toys you push over—he bounces right back again. My boy often cheers me up."

"Is that praise or condemnation, Daddy? Are you accusing me of playing the clown?" Lazarus snatched up three oranges from a bowl and began expertly to juggle. He furrowed his brow in concentration and kept throwing them ever higher. The other two men watched admiringly, if with resignation. They had watched these performances many times before.

Lazarus, ever aware when his audience's interest flagged, piped up again. "Do you know the Pagliacci story?"

"Even if I do, I'd hear it again," said the old man comfortably.

Lazarus kept on juggling, adding in a fourth orange. His face grew pale with effort, but his voice remained light. Years of living abroad in Ireland had given it a musical lilt, if not exactly an Irish accent. His lack of easy breathing had made it perpetually husky as well. "A man is in the depths of despair, you see. He's been depressed for months; finds no reason to go on living. Can't eat, can't sleep. Miserable. He's going to kill himself, he tells his doctor."

"Why on earth would anyone tell his doctor such a thing?" interrupted Warburton.

"Because he wasn't English," snapped Lazarus. "The doctor says, 'Look here, my man. I know the perfect cure for your depression. The great clown Pagliacci is in town this week. You can't help laughing when you see him. He's brilliant! Dazzling. Go watch him perform. I guarantee you'll forget all your troubles.'

"'But doc,' says the man gravely, 'that's the whole problem. I *am* Pagliacci.'"

"Ah." The old man clapped his hands together. "I am Pagliacci! Very good." As an afterthought he added, "But sad."

Lazarus stopped juggling and sank down on the lawn. He did his best to disguise how ill and out of breath he was. "Lord Warburton's case is sadder. He's bored by life. I've never said that—never. I find life only too interesting."

"*Too* interesting. You can't allow it to be that, either, you know."

"Can't help it, Father." Lazarus held his hands out helplessly. "Would you like to see a new card trick?"

"Always," Mr. Sachs answered promptly.

Lazarus removed a pack of playing cards from his breast pocket. His loose lips curved upward, hooked at the ends. His irises were so pale they looked nearly colorless. "Pick a card . . . any card. Take your choice."

"You say that," said his father, deliberating before selecting one. "But it isn't true."

"If you don't like that card, pick another."

"No, I'll stick. You've no excuse for being bored, either of you."

"Remember the card, Daddy. It's no good if you just glance at it and forget it."

"I never forget. When I was your age," Mr. Sachs went on, "I hadn't heard of such a thing as being bored."

"You must have developed late." Lazarus shuffled expertly, with a rattling flourish. "Now put the card in the middle of the pack, please."

"I developed quick—that's my point. When I was your age, I was working twelve hours a day. You wouldn't be bored if you gave yourselves something to do, something that held your interest. You've both got too much time, too much money. Too little at the center."

"I believe it's a black card, am I right?" asked Lazarus, squeezing shut his eyes.

The old man nodded.

"A number card, I think . . . a low number."

"I say, Mr. Sachs," objected Lord Warburton. "You're hardly the man to accuse us of being too rich!"

"Daddy isn't that rich," argued his son. "He's given away vast amounts of money."

"What greater proof of wealth can there be?" asked Lord Warburton, spreading open his hands. He had a large, handsome face and strong forearms, but his hands were small for his size, plump and freckled.

"Focus on your card," Lazarus reminded his father. He snapped his fingers. "I will now make it jump to the top of the pile." He fanned out a handful of cards, all red suits, with only the card on top facing down. "All red—except a single card. Yours, I believe?" He flipped the card and held out the two of spades.

"Wonderful," said the father, sipping his tea in part to hide his delight. "Now show Lord Warburton my favorite trick."

Lazarus groaned. "His favorite is the simplest. Any child could do it with a week's practice." Lazarus hid a card. Revealed it. Turned his hand, so the others could see him hiding it behind his fingers.

"Simplicity is the highest form of art," the old man said. "And of life."

"But leave a little room for beauty," pleaded his son. "For embellishment. And for the beautiful embellishment of untruth when the world becomes too much to bear."

"He's joking again," said Lord Warburton.

"When there are no more jokes, you'll have nothing left," chided Mr. Sachs.

"Fortunately there are always more jokes," said Lazarus.

"I don't believe that," said the old man. "There are serious changes afoot. East Berlin, West Berlin. Korea. Right here in Ireland, despite the good times. The spaces between us are growing—we can't agree on anything. The chasm between rich and poor, differences in religion . . . race . . . point of view. None of it's a laughing matter."

"I agree with you, sir," said Lord Warburton eagerly. "That's just what I've been arguing about with your son."

"Take your British House of Lords, for instance—"

"Exactly!" exclaimed Warburton. When excited, he tended to blush a deep pink-red. "There are serious changes afoot. Some are bound to be very strange indeed. They may do away with the House of Lords altogether—replace it with a House of Ladies," added Warburton, stroking his chin. "I've been mulling over some advice you gave me last month, sir—to devote myself to a purpose, hang my hat on a cause. But one hesitates to take hold of a thing when it's all likely to be blown to smithereens."

"Are we talking about the end of the world again?" groaned Lazarus. He bent down, lifted his smaller dog into the air, and swung it gently from side to side. "What do you think?" he asked the dog. "Are we all going to be blown sky high?"

"I'm not just talking about the atom bomb," said Lord Warburton. "When everything's shifting ground, everything is uncertain."

"Grab hold of a pretty woman," Lazarus suggested.

"The women themselves may be sent flying!" exclaimed Lord Warburton.

"No, the women will stand firm. They may send us flying," said old Mr. Sachs, "but we've had the run of the planet and made a mess of it. The women might save us—at least, the best of them will." He tapped the arm of his chair for emphasis. "I mark a difference between them. Find an interesting woman and marry her, and your life will become much more interesting."

"Yes, but where does one find an interesting woman?" said Warburton. Both listeners were aware that Mr. Sachs himself had not made the luckiest choice in his own marriage. He spent no more than twenty days a year in the company of his wife. Perhaps Mrs. Sachs was fascinating—it was hard to say; she was so seldom present. The two younger men busied themselves around the tea things, and Warburton popped several small scones into his mouth in rapid succession while Lazarus looked on admiringly. The Englishman had a prodigious appetite.

"I wonder what an interesting woman would make of me," Lord Warburton added.

"She'd have to be able to feed you," said Lazarus.

"Fall in love with anyone you please," said the old man, waving one arm, "but not with my American niece."

Lazarus burst out laughing. "Warburton will take that as a challenge. My dear daddy, don't you understand your Englishmen?"

"I don't think I have the honor of knowing your niece," said Lord Warburton. His pale eyes twinkled. "In fact, this is the first I've heard of her. Is she very interesting?"

"We barely know her ourselves," answered Lazarus. "I haven't laid eyes on her since we were small children and went for swims together and things. Come to think of it, she was pretty intriguing then."

"She is recently orphaned," explained Mr. Sachs. "My wife is meeting her in Dublin, against the young lady's objections. She wants to fend for herself."

"Does anyone over the age of twelve count as an orphan?" asked Lord Warburton. "I always picture some vixen with bright-red hair and freckles. I hope she won't be true to type."

"I have heard that her elder Archer cousin back in America has the good looks. Famous for it. This girl seems to be the more independent-minded of the two," said Mr. Sachs.

"Ah—a homely, independent orphan. We can safely bet that Lord Warburton will let her alone," observed Lazarus. He plucked a blade of grass from the lawn and began to chew it.

"When does the young lady in question arrive?" asked Lord Warburton, ignoring his friend.

"It might be any day—or not for weeks," said Lazarus. "My mother communicates by telegram. She doesn't believe in the telephone.

'Changed hotel, very bad, impudent clerk. Niece in hand, quite independent.' We've been puzzling over that. Does she mean 'independent' in a political or a financial sense? Or is she just fond of having her own way?"

"Whatever else, it's sure to mean that," chuckled Warburton.

"I don't envy the hotel clerk," said Lazarus. "My mother must have chewed him up pretty thoroughly."

"Will you at least let me know when this interesting girl arrives?" begged Lord Warburton.

Mr. Sachs swiveled to face him. "Only on condition that you promise not to fall in love with her!"

"Am I such a bad match, really?" pleaded Lord Warburton, his handsome brow furrowed more in bewilderment than worry. He was the catch of the county. And he was not done developing himself; he was still young, he had time. He was one of those rare beings who took an active interest in improving himself.

"I'm sure you are much too fine for my niece," said Mr. Sachs. "I hope she hasn't just come here in search of a husband, as if there were no good men back home. So many American girls do that these days."

"She's sure to be engaged, Daddy," Lazarus put in diplomatically. "American girls usually are."

"Yes," agreed Lord Warburton, "though I can't say it ever makes much difference to *them*. And as to my being too fine, one can but try."

"Try as hard as you like, but don't try charming my niece." Mr. Sachs's sharp old eyes gleamed. "Have you ever been in love, Lord Warburton?"

"No, sir."

"Never? Not even in the Persian Gulf?"

"Nowhere." The young man's smile wobbled slightly.

The look Mr. Sachs gave him was piercing, though not unkind. "Then perhaps you would not suit, after all. You seem to be out of the habit."

Chapter Four

A few weeks later, Lazarus lay dozing in his father's wicker chair, his neck at an awkward angle. The old man used the first hours of the day to dedicate himself to business, but Lazarus had no such pressing occupation. When he was bored, he slept. He woke, startled. No hand touched him, but he felt as if he had been touched.

The figure standing at the edge of the lawn was dressed in black and white, in a dress composed of hundreds if not thousands of tiny dots—like a figure in a Pointillist painting. At first Lazarus thought he might still be dreaming, or inventing visions. But the female apparition, spirit, whatever it was, crossed toward Lazarus's barking dog, walking with quick confident steps. To Lazarus's amazement, she stooped down and in one fluid motion his dog leaped into her waiting arms like a trained circus animal.

"I'm afraid you've just stolen my dog," said Lazarus.

"Can't we share him?" asked the stranger. Her voice was low and musical.

His eyes opened all the way, and he managed to sit up straight. "You may have him altogether."

The young woman approached, still holding the dog. She was wearing white gloves and a small black-and-white hat. Her boldness vanished. "I think I am your cousin, Libby," she said shyly.

Lazarus stumbled to his feet. "I would have said it was settled long ago," he answered. "I'm Lazarus." He swayed a little, unfolding his arms, as if preparing to embrace her, and then at the last minute stuck out a bony arm and shook her hand instead.

"Oh, I know *you*," she cried, juggling the dog in order to accept the handshake. She set the animal gently on the grass, and it pranced around her feet. "You haven't changed a bit."

"I must have been an extremely homely child," said Lazarus drily.

"You were perfectly beautiful," exclaimed his cousin.

"Was I?" he said cynically. But he seemed pleased. His ugly face crinkled into a welcoming smile. "You are American," he said. "And I'm not, really. Not anymore. I don't know quite what to do. Am I supposed to kiss you?"

She laughed. "What would an Irishman do?"

"Oh, he might pat you on the back—after thirty or forty years of close acquaintance."

"I am very glad to see you," she said then, leaning forward and kissing him on the cheek. "Now where is your dear old father?"

"Don't call him a dear old anything," Lazarus advised. "It makes him feel decrepit. He's working in the house. We've been expecting you anytime . . . let me ring him."

His cousin laid one hand on his arm. He was surprised both by the formal white cotton gloves and by the dress, which hung longer than any modern Irish girl's would have done. It made her look old-fashioned, a figure from an earlier era. But the effect was not displeasing—and Lazarus, a good student of humanity, thought perhaps the attractive young lady knew it.

"Oh, you mustn't disturb him," she said quickly. "Perhaps we could sit here alone together a moment till I catch my breath."

"As long as you like," he said. "I was so very sorry to hear about your father," he added. "It must be hard, a loss like that."

"Yes," she said, frowning off into the middle distance, a shimmer of nearly solid green. "It's as if you've been standing in a room leaning on a chair, and someone suddenly took the chair away. I feel off balance."

Lazarus nodded slowly. "I should think it's like having the floor itself taken away," he said.

"Or the room," she agreed. "Or the earth."

His expression was keen, hungry, as if he'd spent too much time alone and it had sharpened his senses. Libby felt her cousin taking her in—her words, her thoughts, almost the air around her. She had washed her hands with lavender soap inside the house; she imagined he could smell the lavender as well.

"There's always the risk of losing everything," he said. They looked at each other a moment. They were friends, in that instant. "Perhaps you'd like a tour of the house?" he asked. "Most people enjoy it."

"Yes please," she said. Her dark eyes were sparkling. "I'd love a tour. Your house is beautiful."

"Is my mother hiding somewhere? Or did she deposit you like a parcel, and then fly off again?"

"She went to her room. She said to please come to her at a quarter to seven precisely."

Lazarus fished out a pocket watch—a handsome, sterling one—and flipped it open. "Mother hates to be kept waiting." He studied his cousin, squinting and tilting his head the way another man might have appraised a painting. "I thought I hadn't remembered you—but as soon as I saw you, it seemed I did. You're very welcome here. We're delighted that you've come."

Libby stood facing the stone front of Gardencourt. All its lines were graceful. The fuchsia were in full bloom, sprays and arches of pinkish-red everywhere. "I think this is the most beautiful place I've ever seen. It doesn't seem real."

"I'm sorry you've gone so long without knowing it." Lazarus shuffled with the stiffness of an old man. "Come—let me show you. Have you had anything to eat? My mother starves people sometimes in her rush to be efficient."

"Not at all. They gave me tea in my room as soon as we arrived. I'm sorry you're in ill health," she added.

"I am dying in bits and pieces," Lazarus said shortly. "But we'll do better, now that you're here. We'll drum up some company to entertain you."

"I'm not worried about being entertained." Libby looked around her, drinking in the peculiar, vivid green of the grass, the rolling downhill pitch toward the Ards Peninsula, and the blue-gray waters beyond. The young woman held her head very erect, Lazarus noticed, and her eyes were alight with interest. She absentmindedly stroked the little dog that frolicked in front of her, courting her attention. He envied the dog. "It's so gorgeous here," she mused. "How funny that I never even knew it existed."

"Yes," said Lazarus, glancing at the landscape appraisingly. "But then, you're very beautiful yourself."

Libby laughed uncomfortably. It was not because she disliked compliments that she took them so badly; on the contrary, they touched her too much and made her uneasy. Often she would remember even the smallest kind remarks years later. Her father had never been lavish in his praise of her, although she remembered him once telling her that she had a sweet voice. She turned away from Lazarus. "Oh yes, *I'm* lovely! How old is your house? Is it Victorian?"

"It's early Tudor," answered Lazarus.

"How funny!" she said. "And are there even older houses nearby?"

"Older, and much grander ones. But don't let my father hear me—he thinks ours is the best place on earth."

"I believe it," she said simply.

Lazarus smiled at her, his rarest, homely smile. "Would you like to see our art gallery? I've chosen most of the paintings myself. But perhaps you need to rest after your travels."

"Oh no!" she said. "I'd love to see the pictures. I don't tire easily. I like to travel. I'd never even been in an airplane before."

"Never been in an airplane?" Lazarus echoed in amazement. "I thought America was a big country. It's enormous compared to Ireland."

"Yes," she said. "But Father didn't enjoy travel. He was . . . we were quite happy where we were."

"In Rochester?"

She stopped walking. He stumbled, then stopped too. His hand on her arm hovered very lightly, as if he were afraid she might break. "Yes," she said decisively. "There are beautiful and interesting things in Rochester too." If she felt hypocritical for defending the place she had just fled, she refused to show it. She might speak ill of her hometown, but she would not allow outsiders to criticize it.

"I'm sorry if I seemed to suggest there weren't. Do you like music at all? We have quite a large record collection."

"I do," she said, relaxing. "But I'm not an expert."

"Well, I am," said Lazarus. "I mean—I live for music. It keeps me sane. But here is our little art gallery." He opened the door to a room filled from floor to ceiling with paintings. The word *little* may have been intended ironically. The pictures had been cleverly arranged, so that it took a second glance to realize how many works of art had been maneuvered into one small space. The gallery occupied an east-facing room, and most of the light had already departed from it, sinking it in gloom. Lazarus fiddled with the overhead lights, adjusting them to arrive at the best possible display.

"Do you care much for modern art?" Lazarus asked, seeing her glance sweep a large, chaotic-looking canvas.

"Isn't all art modern?" asked Libby.

"Actually most art isn't," said Lazarus. "I mean," he added quickly, flushing at the thought he might seem pompous, "most art is either ahead of its time, or what the poets like to call 'timeless.'"

"I see what you mean," she said. "I do like this one, whatever it is."

"He paints with a stick—dripping, instead of a brush."

"Does he?" asked Libby, but her attention had already been captured by a smaller landscape across the room. She strode over to it, Lazarus thought, much as she had done with his dog, with a firm and immediate air of ownership.

"But this one I love," she said.

He stood smiling at the painting, then at his cousin. "You are a good judge. The artist, Garufi, claims he's spent his whole life trying to paint the blue sky."

"A pleasant occupation," answered Libby, standing before it.

"More like an obsession."

"It might be nice to have an obsession," said Libby, her hands clasped behind her back.

"Do you really think so?" Her cousin's eyes were fastened on her.

She smiled. "Well—let us say, a focus. I've lacked that, always."

Lazarus pointed to a nearby quartet of colorful Japanese prints. "Those prints are by Kawase Hasui. I wish I could take one from the frame. You need to see the light shining through it to appreciate what's really there."

As he spoke, Libby Archer stepped into a square of sunlight. The back of her hair lit up gold, while the front of her hair, and her expression, remained in shadow. Her head was bent like a flower on a stem, and for a moment Lazarus felt a sharp pain in his chest. He put one hand over his middle, as if to quell the agony, and Libby looked up, her eyes meeting his.

"Tell me about this one," she said in her low, clear voice, stopping before the portrait of a young woman playing with a small dog.

"That is my favorite," Lazarus said simply. He stepped closer to his cousin. Both bent eagerly toward the painting, and any outside observer would have seen how alike they were that instant.

"The artist painted this when very young," he said. "Seventeen or eighteen, at most. She had no formal training. No prospects, no connections. A famous critic compared her to a dancing poodle. He said the wonder was not that she performed so well, but that she could perform at all."

"People say such stupid things." Libby rested her gloved hand on his arm. There was comfort in her touch. But he did not trust comfort, either. They walked slowly up one side of the hall, looking at more pictures, and down the other, chatting as they strolled. Lazarus did his utmost to keep her entertained—he was at his best telling stories. And Libby was an appreciative audience. He had seldom in his life met one so good. He wondered if she'd had especially sharp schooling, or if she was naturally clever—or a fine actress. He'd met other young women like that. Perhaps his pretty cousin did not care for art or music at all. Everything seemed equally to captivate her attention, her delight. Lazarus did not trust it; he would not trust anything yet.

"I know more about art now than when we began," she said at last. "Will you show the pictures to me again sometime?"

"You have a great passion for knowledge," he observed.

"I'm ashamed of how little most young women know. And I count myself among the ignorant."

"You don't strike me as being like most young women."

"Don't you think so? How many young women do you know?" She turned her sharp gaze on him. "Oh, we could all be better if they gave us the chance! But they won't. They want to lock us up and throw away the key." She gestured at a dark corner of the gallery, gazing into its recesses. "Doesn't this house have a ghost? It should. It's the one thing missing."

"A ghost?" Lazarus echoed.

"A scary, amorphous, haunting thing. We call them ghosts in America."

"So do we here, when we see them."

"So you do see them?" Libby asked eagerly. "You really ought to, in a romantic old place like this."

"This isn't a romantic old place," Lazarus said. "It's dull and prosaic and lonely. There's no romance here except what you've brought in your tartan suitcase."

"How did you know it's plaid?" she asked.

Lazarus shrugged. "We are creatures of our time and place. Had I been less sick, I might have made an excellent spy." Lazarus sank down onto a bench. As if casually, he lay down on his back, his hands behind his head, but there was no disguising the fact that he was done in. He seldom exerted himself this much anymore. The doctors had expressly forbidden it. His lips twisted in an effort to catch his breath.

Libby sat beside him. "Well, I hope to defy my time. But you are right," she added. "I've brought a good deal of romance with me, and it seems to *me* I've brought it to just the right place."

"To keep it out of harm's way, certainly." He tapped one long foot against the other, as if to an invisible beat inside his head. "To protect it."

They were silent awhile. Libby rested her hand on his arm, professionally, as a nurse might. Each time his cousin touched him, his heartbeat seemed to calm.

"Does no one ever come here but you and your father?" Libby asked at length.

"My mother, occasionally."

"She's not terribly romantic."

"Are you bored already? You promised not to be."

"Not at all," said Libby. She smoothed the black dress over her knees. She was blushing.

Lazarus stared up, arms still crossed behind his head. "We see few people, as a rule. My health and my father's don't always allow it. But we will invite all of County Down to meet you, if you like."

"As if I'd let you make yourselves ill over me!"

"It might make us well," said Lazarus. "Shall we drag out the local royalty?"

Libby laughed. "Do you really know kings and queens and lords?"

"Well—a few lords, anyway."

"I am perfectly content just to sit here with you," she told him. "My father's dying was not easy," she added after a moment. "He drank himself to death, slowly." She looked into her relative's homely, upside-down face. "I love that it is quiet and remote here. I find it peaceful."

"Yes, it's like a graveyard," Lazarus said. "But I'm glad you like it. Libby, I hope you never see the ghost."

"So there *is* one!" she cried triumphantly. "I knew there must be."

Lazarus pushed himself up from the bench with something of an effort. He searched his cousin's face. "There are always ghosts," he admitted. "But they're not for everyone. Not for lovely young girls like you. Oh, I know you've suffered a great loss," he added quickly. "I don't mean to make light of your pain. But to see the ghost, you must have suffered long and deeply. To have touched bottom. You need to have come to the end of something—in yourself. I hope you never see the ghost!" he concluded.

"I hope so too," Libby said. "I think people make themselves miserable. We were not made for misery; we were made for life."

"*You* were, I'm sure."

Libby stood abruptly and moved in front of the portrait of the girl and dog. "I'm not just talking about myself!"

"It isn't a flaw, Libby. You're a girl who survived. It's a merit to be strong."

"But if you don't show your suffering, they accuse you of being hard." She could not keep the edge out of her voice.

"And if you do, they call you an idiot. Never mind. The point is to be as happy as possible."

She turned to face him across the hall. "Do you think so? It seems to me there are more important things even than happiness."

"Name one," said Lazarus.

"Well, knowledge. Self-sacrifice. Experience." She hesitated. "Love, I think, may be more important than happiness."

"They aren't necessarily mutually exclusive," her cousin pointed out.

"I suppose not." She smoothed her dress. "I feel as if I've been living inside a box, and I've finally popped open the lid. Should you go see your mother now? Isn't it time?"

"Yes," he said. "I'm glad you are here. As for happiness, I promise I shall contribute to yours in some way." Then, with his hands shoved deep in his pockets as always, he shambled out into the green and empty courtyard.

Chapter Five

Lazarus lay back in the small green boat, watching with half-open eyes as his cousin rowed him to the fringes of the Lough, where green alders and willows made further passage impossible. His hat was pulled down low over his eyes, both to protect him from the sun, to which he was nearly allergic, and to hide his expression, which just now revealed more than he would have liked—gratitude, eagerness, worry, affection, and desperation—none of which ever amounted, never could amount to anything. *Dying men should have poker faces,* he thought.

"Shall I row?" he asked at last.

Libby shook her head and pulled strongly on the oars. She wore her dark hair back in a single, long braid; it made her look like a somber Indian maiden. "You know I can't let you," she said.

"I like to pretend that you could." He let his long fingers trail in the cold current. Though the weather around Strangford stayed mild, thanks to the Gulf Stream, the lake was always bitter cold and smelled of iron. "I'm sorry Father's been so ill lately. It's kept us too much to ourselves."

Libby set off at a slant. The two cousins watched the water sparkle in tiny diamonds as it dripped from the edges of the oar. "I'm glad to be with you. But I'm sorry he's been unwell."

"The gout seems to be moving up from his legs. I don't like the way the doctor talks about it." He frowned, tugging his hat brim down lower. "I've always taken it for granted that Daddy would outlive me."

That was enough to make Libby set down her oars. "What a hope!" she exclaimed. "No parent wishes to outlive their child."

Lazarus dripped lake water from one hand into the other. "I am not an ordinary child," he said. "That has been our tacit agreement, between Daddy and me. We are best friends," he added simply. "I count on him to help me make the best of a bad business. Without him, I don't see—" He shook off the thought, and sent an arc of silver water beads flying. "In any event, let's not talk about health and doctors. We do too much of that around Gardencourt. I was only thinking how few visitors we've been able to arrange."

"But I like those you've had. The Irish are the friendliest people I've ever met. Take Lord Warburton, for instance. I enjoyed him very much."

"You saw him for ten minutes!" Lazarus protested, pushing back his hat.

"I liked what I saw. He seemed a perfect specimen of his kind."

"And he's not Irish at all," Lazarus went on. "He's English—quite a different breed. The Irish and the English! They are as unalike as any two brothers who detest each other. My dear cousin, you'd better not let our neighbors hear you confuse the two."

Libby looked around the vast, quiet expanse of the broad Lough. "There's little danger of that," she said, smiling.

"Oh, the reeds have ears. Don't you know your Greek myths?"

"Not really," Libby said, blushing a little. "I'm not well educated. You'd be shocked by how little I know."

"Nothing about you shocks me," said Lazarus. "Everything delights me."

"You're too easily delighted. I was a mediocre student and stopped too soon. I do have nice handwriting," she added. "But now, my education continues. Tell me the difference between the English and the Irish."

Lazarus laughed. "My dear girl! It would take an encyclopedia."

"Try," she urged him.

He rubbed his chin. "I'm an outsider, you understand," he said. "To both groups. I am, and forever will be, an American . . . and a Jew."

"All the better," Libby smiled. "My father was Christian, you know."

"Yes, that was part of the falling out between our families," said Lazarus. "Some argument over holidays. It's a wonder the human race survives at all." He drew his wet hand across his forehead.

"Are you hot?" she asked anxiously. "Is the sun too strong?" She had made him apply Coppertone before they set out, Lazarus laughing at the Coppertone Girl on the bottle. Libby herself used nothing but baby oil.

"The sun is never too strong in Northern Ireland. . . . Let me think." He closed his eyes. His homely face crinkled in thought; his large, beaked nose seemed to grow larger. "The English are very polite. They are reliably kind. If you get lost in a London street, any one of them can produce a whole book of maps from some mysterious pocket and show you exactly where you need to go. But they won't ever become your friend."

"Never?" asked Libby.

"Not unless you marry in. Perhaps not even then. But an Irishman will shout at you to get the hell out of his way. He may shove you aside. He will tease and torment you, and make rude jokes, and then, if you need it, he'll carry you on his back fifty miles, grumbling all the way."

"It's clear which you prefer."

Lazarus dabbled his fingers in the lake. "We live here. Partly it's the climate, you know. The doctors claimed it would be good for me, and by the time we found out otherwise, it was too late. We had already settled in, put down Irish roots. Daddy loves it here, and so do I. . . . And in all fairness, the English do have scones and clotted cream. We don't."

She pulled on the oars. "Why not?"

"My dear Libby, have you ever eaten an Irish breakfast? If we added scones and cream, we'd be dead before nightfall." He lay back in the boat again, and said musingly, "But it takes a long time to be Irish."

Libby laughed. "I would guess you'd be born into it. That's how it works in America."

Lazarus looked at her seriously. "You might guess it, but you'd be wrong. Irish children are as cruel and indifferent as any other children on earth. But by the time they reach, say, Margaret's age"—Margaret was the name of a favorite kitchen maid, a bright young woman who had featured in many earnest conversations between Lazarus and Libby—"they become loving and kind, thoughtful, and generous to a fault. They become, in short, Irish. But it takes at least twenty years to happen."

"Well, however long it takes"—Libby smiled—"I like them."

"And you also like my father," prompted Lazarus, "though he's every inch an American."

"I do," she declared. "He's the dearest of the dear."

"I won't argue with that," said Lazarus. "And I think you like my mother too, despite her jagged edges."

"I do, because—because—"

Lazarus smiled grimly. "We don't always know why . . ."

"I do!" Libby retorted. "I pride myself on always knowing." She glanced down at her hands, firmly grasping the oars. They were strong, small hands, with beautifully tapered fingers. She wore the gold ring that she had inherited from her mother, a red carnelian stone set into it. In the flashing sunlight it looked like a drop of blood. "I like your mother because she doesn't expect anyone to like her. She doesn't care whether we do or not."

"So you love her out of perversity?" asked Lazarus. "Well, that bodes well for me. I take after my mother," he said, closing his eyes.

"Not at all. You desperately want people to like you, and try your hardest to make them. You cavort and make jokes and do magic tricks till they stop and pet you."

"Good Lord, how you see through me!" Lazarus cried, with mock dismay.

"But there are limits," Libby added more soberly. "You don't really let a person draw close. I don't know what's wrong with you exactly, but I think you're a great fake."

Lazarus gave a smile that was more of a grimace. "You mean you don't think I'm ill? It's handy to think so."

"Oh no . . . no! I know you are very unwell." She regretted her words immediately. Libby spoke her mind too freely—she had been told this more than once—but she hated the idea of causing injury. Her father had compared her once to a scalding light—she illuminated her object, he complained, but left one feeling exposed and helpless. She had never forgotten it. She tried to soften and dim down the lamp, but often failed. "I just meant that I don't know what you really care for. I'm not sure you care for anything at all."

"I care only for you, dear cousin," said Lazarus, placing one hand over his heart.

"I'd like to believe even that." She pointed an oar at him, dripping water into the boat. "You sharpen your wit on everything: your miserable life; religion; politics; philosophy . . . it's all comic material for you. And you never do stop," she added. "You never stop performing for an instant."

"I keep a lively band playing in my antechamber, Libby." He tapped his bony forehead. "It plays without ceasing. Very handy. One, it keeps the noise outside from reaching the inner apartments, and two, it makes the world think there's always dancing within." He danced his thin white fingers along the edge of the boat.

"I would like just once to enter the private apartment, as you put it."

"No you wouldn't." He shook his head so hard a lank strand of white hair fell into his eyes from under the brim of his hat, like the ghost of a leaf. "It's a dismal place. Trust me."

Just then a bell sounded from the depths of the Gardencourt grounds. This sonorous outdoor bell was used only on rare occasions—to summon large numbers of guests to meals, or to signal urgency or danger. It had once been used to call residents to prayer in the now-unused private chapel. "Saved by the bell!" Lazarus laughingly exclaimed. "Now why on earth is Warburton using that thing?"

He sat up straighter in the boat and waved his arm at a distant fair-haired figure standing on the back lawn of the mansion.

"There's your perfect specimen of an Englishman," he told his cousin. "What good timing he has!"

"He's almost too perfect." Libby swung the boat gracefully around and headed dutifully for home.

"Heavens yes," said Lazarus. "*Ecce homo!* Look at his white flannels." He shook his head with admiration. "Not a speck of dirt on him, I'll bet."

"You mean all the English are like him?" asked Libby in a low voice. She was unsure how well sound carried.

"Oh no. They're not all like Lord Warburton. He's so exactly the best copy he's almost an original."

Libby leaned forward to take a better look. The gentleman in question was striding toward them at an alarming pace. Seconds earlier he had looked like a toy soldier. Now they could make out the broad smile on his face. "Come along!" he called impatiently.

Lord Warburton paced by the bank, now larger than life. Suddenly, like some sort of water animal, he splashed in his boots into the Lough to help pull the small boat to shore. He did this in spite of all of Libby's protests and despite Lazarus's angry stream of jokes and taunts. He lifted Libby out of the boat as if she were a child, holding her around the waist and lifting her into the air, then setting her down on the grassy bank beyond the reeds. From no one else on earth would Libby have tolerated such behavior, but Lord Warburton was not anyone else on earth; it would have seemed petty not to accept his assistance, so cheerfully and matter-of-factly given.

Lazarus, scorning all help, flapped his hand and waded to shore, half stumbling and half swimming as he went. By the time he'd achieved dry land he was soaking wet, his trousers streaming with lake water.

"I'm heading in to get changed," he called irritably over his shoulder, as he marched past his friend and his cousin toward Gardencourt. Libby gazed after him sympathetically, but Warburton just grinned, showing white teeth.

"I hope you've been keeping well?" said Lord Warburton, looking at his pretty companion.

"Yes, thank you," said Libby. She still retained the sensation of having recently flown through the air in the arms of a nearly perfect stranger. Her canvas shoes were damp but she was otherwise dry. She wore a pair of pedal pushers and a striped T-shirt, clothing that felt woefully inadequate beside Lord Warburton's cream-colored suit. He looked like something out of an ad—but an advertisement for something she had never yet seen. *So this,* she thought, *this is Europe.*

"I see you've been rowing your cousin about. Of course *he* doesn't row—he's far too lazy."

Libby glanced after her cousin's receding back. Lazarus could not have overheard, yet she lowered her voice. "He has good reason for what you call his laziness," she said.

"Ah, Lazarus has a good excuse for everything!" Lord Warburton retorted with a laugh.

Lazarus stopped walking and turned. He called, "My excuse for not rowing is that my cousin does it so beautifully! She touches nothing that she doesn't improve." Then he opened the parlor door and disappeared inside.

Warburton regarded Libby more closely. His small blue eyes twinkled. "It makes one want to be touched, Miss Archer."

~

Warburton stayed on for tea, and then supper, and finally declared himself willing to spend the night. This was a coup, as Lazarus confided to his mother, because Warburton was so extremely fond of his own house that he seldom ventured abroad unless forced to by business or duty. This was a well-known fact. The next day he extended his stay till the end of the weekend. Mrs. Sachs was pleased—it was a victory for Gardencourt. She had a secret fondness for the nobility, which she would sooner have died than admitted. She regarded her niece with new appreciation. Mr. Sachs was delighted, because Warburton kept his son lively. And Lazarus believed he was at last being a good host to his American cousin. He could have wished Libby a little less impressed by his English friend; he could have wished Warburton a little more circumspect in his admiration—but he chalked this up to his own bad character, the usual ill humor of an invalid.

"I can hardly expect to keep her all for myself," he reminded himself. "I must be other-regarding, other-regarding, other-regarding."

"What are you mumbling about?" Warburton asked him. "Have you taken up praying?"

"The greatest prayer is patience," Lazarus replied.

Warburton had a quiet way of making himself the center of attention. He did it without bragging; in fact, he seldom said much in company. He acted much like the sun; he could not help shining, and he wasn't responsible if others naturally orbited around him, soaking in his warmth. Even Mr. Sachs, who had lately been so ill, suddenly regained his spirits and his appetite. The cook, learning that Lord Warburton was their houseguest, became newly inspired, and Margaret, the housemaid, gawked at the big, handsome, healthy visitor, with his gold cufflinks and Dunhill embossed leather card case. Margaret, a "mere broth of a girl," as she herself said, usually wore her hair up in curl papers under a cap, except once a week when her fellow took her to the movies. But with Lord Warburton visiting, Margaret carefully combed and styled her hair each day.

When the weather held fine they sat out of doors. In the evening, they retired to the spacious rooms within. Lord Warburton was warm in his praise of Gardencourt, though he reserved his highest praise for his own estate, Greyabbey, a few kilometers north of the Strangford Lough, near Newtonards.

"It's the most beautiful place in the world," he told Libby. "You must come see it."

"Nonsense!" said Mr. Sachs. "It's an old ruin compared to Gardencourt."

Libby stood close to Margaret, who smiled, shook her head, and confided in a low voice, "Oh, Greyabbey's the finest house in County Down. The very finest, miss. I've always longed to have a peek inside."

Libby turned at once. "We'll come then, if we can bring Margaret," she said.

"Oh no, miss!" declared Margaret, with horror.

"Just as you wish," said Lord Warburton with a smile.

"Margaret is the only one who can keep my uncle comfortable when he is away from home," said Libby. Then, flustered, she apologized to her aunt. "I'm sorry, I meant—"

"We all know what you mean," returned her aunt, a bit stiffly.

"I hope you all will come," said Warburton gallantly. "It's a curious old place."

"Has it got ghosts?" asked Libby.

"Oh, loads of them."

"Do you come from a large family?" Libby asked Lord Warburton when they had a moment alone. She prided herself on wanting to learn something about everyone.

"About average," he answered. "One younger brother in the church, and one older brother still in the army. Two sisters who live at home—our parents are gone. My mother died very young, and my father followed not long after. None of us is very clever, you know, Miss Archer, but we're all perfectly pleasant. I hope you'll come to know us well."

"I don't know if I will be in Ireland long enough to know anyone well," said Libby. She felt uncomfortable. She was not directing the conversation as she'd wished.

"Are you planning to leave us so soon?" Lord Warburton did not disguise his disappointment. "Do you love America so much that you have to rush back to it?"

"I love my country pretty well," said Libby. "I feel as if I know it better for having a little distance from it. All things considered, I think it is the best place on earth."

Lord Warburton laughed, then sipped his lemonade to cover his laughter. "Most of your countrymen seem to feel that way," he amended.

"I don't know most of my countrymen," she said. "I do like the idea of a democracy. And we don't seem to have as many classes as you do here. I suppose you must have about fifty."

"I don't believe in the class system," said Warburton. "All that is rubbish. I go in only for equality."

"Easy to say when you own a good slice of the country," observed Lazarus from across an open expanse of grass.

"I don't own a good slice," argued Warburton apologetically. "It's a very small slice, really." He held his palms close together to demonstrate. "We have a parliamentary government back home in England," he said.

"Yes, so I've heard," teased Libby. "I also think you have a king and queen?"

"Mostly for show," said Warburton.

"And do you dine with them often?" she asked.

"Dine with them?" he echoed.

"Yes, the king and queen. Or don't they go in for equality the same way you do?"

"Oh, I say, Miss Columbia." He looked both dismayed and amused, and stood swirling the ice around in his drink, staring into the glass.

"He really has dined at Windsor, you know," put in Lazarus wickedly. "Perhaps he can get you invited."

"If only I'd known, I'd have brought my native costume," said Libby.

❧

Mr. Sachs retired very early. He hid his illness from the others as best he could—though the anxious eye of his son could not be fooled.

Half an hour later, Mrs. Sachs turned to Libby with a decisive nod. "It's time to bid the gentlemen goodnight." She had been sorting through her calling cards. Though not an especially sociable woman, she loved getting calling cards, and grumbled when she felt the pile was insufficiently high. In the isolated Ards, it was almost not worth the bother.

"Must I, Aunt?" pleaded Libby. "It's not even dark yet. We're having such a nice time. I'll come up in an hour."

"I can't possibly wait that long," said Mrs. Sachs, her voice sharp. She disliked anything that reminded others of her age. "It may be light out, but it's past my bedtime."

"You don't need to wait up. Lazarus and I will tidy up here. We'll close all the cupboard doors and turn out the lights, just as you like."

"I'll turn out the lights with you!" Lord Warburton exclaimed. He was standing with his back to the fireplace, his legs spread apart. "Please let me. Only promise that you won't think of going to bed before midnight."

Mrs. Sachs fixed her bright, critical eyes on him a moment, and then moved them coolly to her niece. "You can't stay alone here with two men, Libby. You're not in Rochester anymore."

Libby rose at once, blushing. After a moment she exclaimed, "I wish I were!"

"Mother," chided Lazarus. "Good Lord, I am her cousin. You might go easy on us."

Mrs. Sachs turned a cold look on her son. "I was not aware that Lord Warburton was our relation."

"My dear Mrs. Sachs," said Lord Warburton. "I can certainly remove myself, if I am in the way."

"I didn't invent the rules or the customs of the country," said Mrs. Sachs, "I must take them as I find them."

Warburton gave a small bow. "I am happy to retire early," he said.

"Nonsense," protested Lazarus, with an appealing gesture. "You are our guest. We won't send you off to bed before dark. Mother, please!"

Mrs. Sachs rolled her eyes and sank back down in despair. "Oh, for heaven's sakes. Fine then. I'll just sit here and stay up till midnight."

"You'll do nothing of the kind," said Libby, as if nothing had ever ruffled her. "We'll go up together now."

Lazarus watched his cousin for signs of temper. She seemed calmer and more self-possessed than ever. She bid the young men a cordial goodnight, but said nothing to her aunt as they climbed the long stairs, covered in a richly figured crimson oriental pattern.

At the top of the landing, still in silence, Libby turned to go.

"You are angry with me for interfering," said Mrs. Sachs.

Her niece paused before her bedroom door. "I'm not angry," Libby said slowly. "But I am confused. Was it so bad that I wanted to stay down in the drawing room?"

"It just isn't done, not in this part of the world. Young women here, the decent ones, do not sit alone with young men late at night. "

Libby took this in for a moment. "You were right to tell me then," she said. "I'm glad to know the right thing."

"I will always tell you when I see you taking liberties," said her aunt.

"I hope you will. But I may not always agree."

Mrs. Sachs smiled tautly. "I expect you won't. You're a modern young woman. And you are awfully fond of having your own way."

"Most people are fond of their own way. But I need to know what I'm not supposed to do." Libby rested one hand lightly on the doorknob.

"So as to do it anyway?" asked her aunt with a sardonic smile.

"So as to *choose*," said Libby, turning the doorknob and slipping into her room.

Chapter Six

The visit to Greyabbey was quickly arranged. Mr. Sachs, though rebounding from his recent illness and confined to a wheelchair, was eager to make the journey—"I want to see these so-called improvements," the old man declared—and Margaret, as promised, came along to help out. Mrs. Sachs made herself unavailable. Old Irish houses bored her. Old Irish houses even when owned by English nobility were not much better—and she had friends from Italy visiting less than an hour's drive away.

Though it was midsummer, Greyabbey was large, dim, and cool as a vault, and drafty enough that a fire in the large fireplace was welcome in August. Mr. Sachs sat in the great hall, with his shawl over his legs and a cup of tea in his hands. Libby, who was standing just beside her uncle, shivered in her lightweight cotton shift.

"What do you think of our host?" old Mr. Sachs asked his niece.

"I think he's charming," she answered promptly.

"Yes, he's a nice fellow, but please don't fall in love with him."

Her lips twitched into a smile. "I will wait for your recommendation before I fall in love with anyone," said Libby. "I'm not in a rush. Besides, your son seems to think Lord Warburton is an eccentric."

"The British are an eccentric race. Most are hopeless romantics at bottom. At the top, it's another matter. They appear to have a thin layer of ice. Brave, though. Look how they've just survived another war. But there's no shortage of forward thinkers among the nobility these days. Of course, Warburton's radicalism is almost entirely theoretical. He wouldn't let them touch a stone of Greyabbey." He lowered his voice confidentially. "I heard he sat in a chair and watched the bricklayers lay out that new entrance of his, brick by brick. Drew it out in advance, exactly the way he wanted it, even to the shades of brick."

"Well, that sounds odd to *me,*" said Libby.

"Yes . . . Americans are dedicated to the *idea* of perfectibility. But we are less interested in actual perfection. That takes too much work. We are happiest when we are living among the clouds—like Emerson, with his head bathed in the ether and so on. The English are cheeriest grubbing out old roots in their gardens. Now, here are two more perfect examples," he said, inclining his head toward two young ladies who had materialized at the top of the broad, stone interior stairs. They giggled shyly with their heads together like two schoolgirls.

Except, on second glance, they were not girls. They might have been middle-aged, or at least in their early thirties. Both wore shirtwaists made of Liberty cotton lawn, covered in millefiori patterns. The fairer and taller of the two wore cornflower blue. The other, a little plumper, dark red. They suddenly stood stock-still, like deer that have been spotted.

Lord Warburton appeared, throwing one arm around each of them, squeezing one shoulder at a time. "Here are my sisters, Katherine and Birdy," he announced. The tall, fair sister was Katherine and the shorter, rounder one, Birdy. They regarded their brother adoringly. Libby had never seen such worshipful gazes, and she determined to see what lay underneath.

The sisters offered Libby a tour of the summer gardens after lunch. They walked with parasols over their heads, like beings from another century. Stout Birdy knew the name of every flower and shrub. And when Katherine stood still, a bright-red bird flew to her shoulder and stayed a moment, regarding Libby with one black, beady eye before it flew away.

"Is he kind to you, always, your brother?" asked Libby, beginning her cross-examination.

Both sisters regarded her with wide-open faces.

"Oh yes," breathed Birdy.

"You can't imagine how kind," said Katherine. "People don't know how much good he does—they simply don't have any idea."

"He seems to me to be an awful tease," said Libby provocatively.

Birdy looked away, but Katherine blushed.

"And I wonder," said Libby, "if he isn't pretending."

"Pretending?" echoed Katherine faintly. She folded her hands high over her chest and held them there, gazing helplessly at her strange guest.

"He is completely genuine, isn't he, Katherine?" said Birdy, as if Libby weren't there. "And he's been decorated, twice—though he never speaks of it, and he'd be angry if he knew I had mentioned it."

"But would he really give"—and here Libby made a sweeping gesture with her hand, to take in the gardens, and the high stone towers of Greyabbey, and the cottages, fields, and hills beyond—"all this away? Would he give it all up?" She was recalling her conversation with him.

"Because of the expense, do you mean?" breathed Katherine, while Birdy just stared at their guest. "I suppose," Katherine went on faintly, "he might let out a few of the houses, if it came to that."

"Let them for nothing? To whoever needed them most?" demanded Libby.

"I don't understand," Katherine said.

"Your brother's a great radical, I thought," said Libby.

"Oh!" said Katherine. "Yes, Alfred is very advanced."

"But he's always rational," said Birdy. "He's not some cuckoo, if that's what you're wondering."

"Not at all," put in Katherine.

"But if I were you—I mean all of you—I would fight to the death to defend and claim it. All of this." Her sweeping arm took in the greenish-gray scenery, its rising mists, and the blue sky sparkling between mottled clouds. "Why should you let anyone take it? What better use are they going to put it to? Things once taken apart are usually destroyed, aren't they?"

"But we have always been liberal people," said Katherine.

"Oh yes," Birdy agreed. "Going back hundreds and hundreds of years."

They were interrupted by shouting, cries of laughter, and more shouting. The two sisters listened intently, then took to their heels, pounding across the grass, their Liberty shirtwaists flapping around their legs.

"Good heavens, it's the vicar!" cried Birdy.

"Not a moment's notice!" Katherine called back.

"Typical, typical!"

Libby trotted after them. Her skirt was cut narrow, not full like theirs, and she had worn sharp little heels that day, which cut into the furze and wanted to stick there. By the time she caught up, she saw Lord Warburton fending off the attack of some fair-haired stranger, roaring and charging at him, butting him with his head. The new man was a few inches shorter, but broader built, with immense shoulders. He wore a collarless white shirt.

"In the name of our Lord, have at me!" called the attacker. "Do it in Jesus's name!"

"I'm wearing my best suit!" protested Warburton. He braced himself for the next tackle.

"Do it with heart! With heart, I command you."

"Is that really a vicar?" asked Libby in amazement.

Birdy turned her head. She was smiling. "Yes, it's our brother!" she answered.

Warburton had now caught sight of Libby, and his expression changed. He stepped forward with a look of determination—did something with his foot—and the vicar landed upside down on the lawn, howling in outrage.

"Foul play!" he shouted. "You swept me with your leg. I swear! I've never seen you do that, never—" Something in his brother's look made him turn around. He spotted Libby as well, and scrambled to his feet, reaching for a purple surplice lying crumpled nearby and throwing it on hastily over his head. Katherine darted forward to straighten it, tugging on the hem, as if she were dressing a boy in his nightshirt.

"Oh Christ our Lord, I didn't realize we had female visitors. Forgive me. Very nice to meet you! I'm the idiot brother, Charles." He put out one wide hand, realized it was smeared with dirt and grass, and wiped it on his purple robe.

Warburton stepped in and made introductions all around.

"Jesus." The vicar tugged at his own thick mop of hair. "You must think I'm glocky."

The elderly Mr. Sachs, arriving in his wheelchair from the manor house, where he'd been contentedly studying the china patterns, looked to his son. Lazarus spun his finger beside his head.

"Charles used to be a wrestler," Lord Warburton explained. "Best in five counties."

"Best in the North of Ireland," said Katherine.

"Best on the Emerald Isle," said Birdy. "No one in the south ever pinned our Charlie."

"Now I'm a man of the cloth and hammered for life," said the vicar.

"Married," Birdy explained.

"With three strapping boys. While my poor big brother languishes up here all alone on his hill, like a vestal virgin. It's not right. It's not healthy."

"Oh no," said Lord Warburton, shaking his head, his face going purple with embarrassment. "Don't. Please don't."

"Everything to do with the soul comes through the body," persisted the vicar. "You cannot have the one whole without the other fully intact. Look at me!" he proclaimed, gesturing at his broad chest. "I grant you, I've a bit of a gut, but at least I'm not wasting my essence in the bloody House of Lords."

"Oh, Charles," said Katherine faintly. "Must you speak of such things in front of company?"

"Wouldn't you like to see the pond?" Warburton asked Libby desperately. "It's fully stocked with carp this time of year. Beautiful creatures." He put out his hand and pulled her away.

"Right!" Lazarus called after him. "Leave *us* here with the Sermon on the Mount."

"You mean the Sermon *of* the Mount!" boomed back the vicar with a laugh while the two sisters chirped their disapproval.

Warburton clutched Libby's arm firmly and dragged her out of earshot. They climbed up and down a few small hills till they stood gazing down at a sizable lake, brimming with blue water and fringed with alders. As if he had just realized that they were still touching, he released Libby's arm and gestured at the scene below. "Pond," he announced, unnecessarily. Then after a moment, his long legs akimbo, he added, "I suppose all families are a little mad."

"Yours seems rather nice," she said.

He glanced at her, then away. "I should like you to really get to know this place properly. There's more to it—more to *us*—than meets the eye."

"I should like that," she answered, hardly knowing what she said.

"Ah, I'm glad to hear you say that, Miss Archer. It charms me when you say that."

Libby traced with the toe of her shoe a semicircle over the grass where they stood, as if drawing with a writing instrument. "I fear you are too easily charmed."

"No," he said. "I'm not easily charmed. But you have charmed me."

Libby straightened, sensing a familiar danger. She seemed very American in that moment, and any one of a number of magazine editors writing on the propriety of women in this day and age would have been proud of her. Her expression was watchful, her hazel eyes bright but cool. "I'm afraid it may be impossible for us to visit again, however," she went on quickly. "We'll be leaving for the Continent soon. My aunt spends most of her time abroad, and I am in her hands."

The water made small plashing noises. A golden fish leaped into the air and fell again into the blue depths. "I don't believe that," said Lord Warburton. "You strike me as someone whose fate is entirely in her own hands."

"I'm sorry to give a false impression," she said. "I've never met anyone whose fate was entirely in their own hands. I don't believe such a person exists. And if they did," she added more passionately, "it would not be a young woman in my position, living in the 1950s—or at any time within human memory."

"Is your position such a poor one?" he asked gently. The question hung in the air. Both of them blushed, and they moved a little farther apart. "I'm sorry," he said. "I didn't mean to pry . . ."

"I hate being an object of pity, and I've found myself in that position so often lately. I can't reconcile myself to it." She shook her head ruefully. "I should become one of those nuns who live in the caves in France."

"That would be a terrible waste," said Warburton. "I hope you won't give up on humanity altogether—there are one or two corners of it still worth saving." He picked up a flat stone at his feet and skimmed it across the pond. The air smelled like salt from the sea. The stone skipped once, twice, three times. "This place, for instance." He turned to face her, hands at his sides. "My brother's right. I spend too much time alone on that hill. But outside the company of my sisters, and a few good hunting dogs, I'm never at ease in the world. London seems like a gigantic gray beehive to me—full of buzzing."

"You must find it peaceful here," said Libby, trying not to make too much of his lumping his sisters together with his hunting dogs.

"I do," he said. After a long pause he added, still awkwardly, "I think you would find it peaceful too."

"I do," she replied. Then they both blushed again. There was a cloudiness in the air, like the lull before rain. Her host was trying to convey . . . something that he was not saying. Libby, to hide her confusion, bent and picked up a small, smooth black stone. She held it up to show him.

"You're never far from the sea here," he said, pocketing the black stone, "but I'm afraid you must find this place very provincial and dull, after New York. I'm afraid you despise us."

"Despise you?" she asked.

"Yes." He picked up another flat rock and threw it from him as if trying to get rid of it. It flashed across the pond six times before it sank out of sight. Insects chirped in the grass, singing like birds.

"Of course I don't despise you," she said. "You've been lovely to us. You, and your sisters—"

"Yes." He simply stood a moment, looking at her. There was a gentle, hopeless expression on his face, and then he shrugged. "I hope at least you'll let me come to Gardencourt to say goodbye before you go. I'd like to speak privately. May I come and see you one day next week?"

"You are a family friend. I don't see how I could prevent you."

"I don't feel safe with you, Miss Archer. I have a sense that you're always judging people, summing them up."

"Well, if I'm a good judge, and you have nothing to hide—"

"But why judge people at all? Why not just let them be?" He turned his head as if he could hear something at a distance. Yes, there was the barking of one of his retrievers. "We're being rude. We should head back." He strode ahead of her, his long legs scissoring through the grass. But he held one hand on the small black stone in his pocket, as if it were a promise he meant to keep.

Chapter Seven

The phone rang close to Lazarus's sleeping head. His room was dark and chilly. He pushed the heavy black receiver off its cradle. He spoke into the receiver. "Who in God's name is calling at this hour?" he demanded.

"It's after eight a.m.," exclaimed a clear female voice. The accent was obviously American. "You must be the sick cousin!"

"You must be . . ." His voice trailed off, and he sat up in bed, drawing the covers around his naked shoulders. "I give up," he said. "Who is this?"

"I'm Libby's best friend," said Henrietta. "Didn't you get my telegram? Henrietta. I've just arrived in Belfast. I had to get the money straightened out, and my boss at the Rochester newspaper was being awfully cheap."

"What telegram?" asked Lazarus. He fumbled around with his fingers for a pack of cigarettes, drew out a cigarette, and lit it.

"Are you joking?" she cried. "I checked three times to make sure it went through. *Three times.*"

"I am joking," said Lazarus. "We'll send a car to fetch you and your elderly great-aunt. You've flown together into Belfast, haven't you?"

"Oh, good news. I'm traveling solo," said Henrietta crisply. "My great-aunt passed away."

Lazarus was silent a moment, exhaling smoke. He picked a bit of tobacco from his lips. "That *is* good news," he said in a dry voice.

"Sorry to sound heartless. You don't know me. And you didn't know her. She was not a nice person. And she was very old. Almost ninety-four, though she lied about her age. She died crossing the street against traffic."

"Served her right then," Lazarus said.

"I don't suppose Libby is there, is she? *She* would be wide awake at this hour. At least she would be awake at home. In America, I mean."

"Libby tells me you're very patriotic," said Lazarus, looking around for an ashtray. When he couldn't find one, he perched his cigarette on a small statue of a fox above the bed, placing it between the animal's marble ears.

"Yes, and proud of it!" Henrietta exclaimed. She raised her voice. She didn't trust the quality of non-American phone equipment. She was standing inside a bright-red phone booth, and a line had formed outside her booth. She turned her back firmly to the crowd and straightened her hat.

"I could hunt for my cousin if you need her," said Lazarus. "Or you could be a good girl and just tell me where to send the car."

"Please don't call me a good girl," said Henrietta. "You are Libby's relation and I think we should try to get along. Don't you?" She didn't wait for him to answer. "All right then, why don't you send the car to Great Victoria Street. Thanks. I'll be waiting."

Lazarus put up the big black umbrella and made sure that Libby was securely under it before he steered her toward the crowded Great Victoria train station. It had been fine out in the country, but it was raining on Great Victoria Street, a sleety autumn rain that held a thinly veiled threat of hail. It was raining in Belfast; of course, it always rained in Belfast.

"I'm going to hate your friend," Lazarus had said gloomily as they entered the station through one of its many arched gray doorways. The place smelled of diesel, and fried potatoes, and the sweeter scent of nearly decaying damp wool. Lazarus wore a thin cardigan sweater with elbow patches. "I may as well dress the part of the Irishman," he had told Libby. "I only wish I had one of those wool caps the old men wear."

"You will love her, if only for my sake," said Libby now, distracted, for she had already begun trying to pick out the tall, lean figure of her friend in the busy station.

"I cannot love even for your sake," said Lazarus, buckling the big black umbrella closed and shaking off the excess rain. "Or stop loving, for that matter." The station had high, webbed, vaulted glass-and-steel ceilings that made sounds bounce from one corner to the other. It looked like the underside of a bridge. "I suppose we're looking for some battle-ax dressed head to toe in brown Macintosh? You needn't tell me she's homely, for I've already heard her speak."

"Henry is beautiful," answered Libby, between annoyance and amusement. "And she dresses far better than I do."

"Women always stick up for each other," Lazarus said.

But Libby had spotted Henry. "See," she said and pointed.

As if she had picked out the sound of her friend's voice from all other noises—train whistles, heels clacking, engines emitting puffs of steam—Henry swiveled around and spotted Libby. She was indeed dressed elegantly, in a rose-red dress with a ruffle at the neck. She was clutching a small white bouquet of violets, but when she saw Libby moving toward her, she threw her arms open with a dazzling smile.

Lazarus whistled between his teeth.

Henry froze. Her eyes flashed—he could see that even at this distance, and he watched her taking his measure—his bony figure, his trembling fingers, the hair prematurely white. A look of pity rolled across her face like a cloud, then hid itself. She bared her teeth in a grin and dropped a small, mocking curtsy.

❧

Back in Gardencourt, Henrietta and Libby sat ensconced in the drawing room, with old Mr. Sachs and Lazarus dancing attendance, and Margaret pouring the tea. A crackling fire sent a few sparks up into the flue. The room smelled of wood smoke and cake.

"I can't believe this is September," said their guest. "Rochester was stifling, still." Henrietta balanced her tea and cake plate on her long, silk-stockinged legs. She looked, Lazarus was thinking, like a racehorse stuck indoors. He envied Henry her energy and at the same time it exhausted him to the point where now and again he lay back his head and closed his eyes. It would be easy enough to fall in love with a girl like Henrietta—if he were in the market for love.

"But this is very pleasant," she added hastily.

"I'm glad you like it," said Lazarus, with his eyes closed.

"How much did this place cost you?" Henry asked Mr. Sachs.

"Henry!" cried Libby.

"Are we not allowed to talk about money?" said Henry innocently.

"You may talk about anything you please," said Mr. Sachs.

"Yes—would you like to know how much we weigh?" asked Lazarus.

"I would like to know how much you pay your servants," said Henrietta, as soon as Margaret had stepped out of the room.

"Why not call them slaves, and assume we pay nothing at all," suggested Lazarus.

"I'm so sorry," said Libby, rubbing her forehead with her knuckles.

"All right, all right," said Henry in a slightly grumpy voice. She drank her tea. "Is this what they call Irish tea?" she asked.

"Yes," said Libby.

"What makes it Irish, exactly?"

The two Sachs men stared at her mutely.

"It's made of potatoes," said Lazarus at last.

"Never mind," said Henry, drawing a small notebook and silver pen from her large, rectangular-shaped handbag. "I'll look it up later. That's the sort of detail our readers want to know."

"Your readers?" said Mr. Sachs faintly.

"Miss Capone is a journalist, Daddy," said Lazarus. "You remember. She's going to earn a Pulitzer exposing us."

"But seriously," said Henrietta, "can you introduce me to some of the local nobility? And of course I'd like to meet some of the common people too."

"You mean the peasants?" said Lazarus.

Henrietta studied him over the rim of her teacup, her eyes very large and a surprisingly beautiful, dark shade of green. "How long has it been since you've visited your native land?" she asked.

"I haven't been back to America in ages," said Lazarus. "I doubt they miss me."

"But you can't know, can you, till you go. Perhaps if you touched your own soil, you would spring back to life and strength like Antaeus."

"I thought you were a journalist, Miss Capone, not a writer of fables."

"It is not a fable that we each represent our civilization," she answered.

"Heaven forbid that I should represent anything!" Lazarus exclaimed.

Henry looked at him with her lips pursed. "Well, perhaps you are right," she murmured, putting her pen and notebook down. She dug a fork into her cake, but hesitated before eating it. "Still I think we all have something to contribute to this world—if we can find our passion."

"I agree with you there," Mr. Sachs said warmly. "I've been telling my son exactly that for ages."

Henry took her pen and scribbled a few lines into her notebook. She put the pen and paper back inside the dark reaches of her large bag, and balancing the cup and plate awkwardly, as before, picked up her fork. "And is this Irish cake?" she asked.

"Yes, it's also made of potatoes," answered Lazarus.

Libby exchanged an agonized glance with Mr. Sachs's amused one. "Will they go on like this all week?" she asked him.

"I hope so," said the elderly gentleman.

Upstairs, alone in her room with her friend, Henrietta unpinned her long hair and began to brush it, slowly and steadily. "I have something important to tell you," said Henry. "You haven't asked me a thing yet about Cap Lockwood."

"Haven't I?" asked Libby, her voice too high. She shook out a silk dress belonging to Henry and hung it at the front of the closet, fastening the top button in place.

"God, I hate wearing stockings," Henry announced, suddenly throwing down her brush and removing her nylons, rolling them down from the top and tossing them onto the bed. "Do you know there's a woman named Fogarty writing about *wife dresses*? She tells women never to leave the house without a girdle."

"I've never worn one," said Libby. "Are they as uncomfortable as they look?"

"I wouldn't know," said Henry, "but my great-aunt lived and died in one. She was wearing it in her hospital bed the day she passed away. But don't shift subjects on me, Libby. Don't you care at all what happens to that man?" She picked up her hairbrush again and waved it in the air.

"What man?" asked Libby. She stayed standing in the closet, breathing in the strong scent of cedar. It was a smell she associated with her childhood and visiting horse stalls with her father at the Saratoga race track. A smell of danger, mixed with gin, in those days.

"Cap is coming here after you," said Henry, brushing her hair again in short, definite strokes. "Thirty-six, thirty-seven, thirty-eight," she said, counting aloud. "I hoped you'd be pleased to know he still cares enough to come."

Libby turned. Her face was pale and stern. "What do you mean, coming after me? I'm not some runaway. Couldn't you tell him not to come?"

"When has anyone been able to tell Cap anything?" Henry laid down the brush. "He just wants to see you, assure himself you're all right. I thought you were such good friends, Libby. What happened before you left?"

"He doesn't need any more friends apparently." Libby could not keep the bitterness out of her voice.

"Well, if he said so, that wasn't kind. But people say unkind things when they are hurting . . . when they want something they can't have. I don't know why we insist that human beings are so elevated. I've never known a dog to hold a grudge—or a horse, or a cat." She resumed brushing her hair, counting under her breath. After a moment she added in her journalist's voice, "Do you really feel you could never love him? If so, I guess you'd better tell him and get it over with, so you can both move on. He's considered a great catch, you know, and a business genius. I'm sure he'll find someone to love eventually."

Libby kicked off her shoes. "I hope so," she said. "I want him to be happy." Henry swung around in her chair and regarded her friend, unblinkingly.

"Do you really?" said Henry. "Be very sure, Libby, before you send him packing."

"I wonder if men get married just to get it over with," said Libby. "If they reach a certain age and think to themselves, 'I need a wife,' the way they would say, 'I need a suit.' Or a house, or a car. Then they look for a likely candidate."

"I have no idea," said Henry. "I've never been a likely candidate, so I can't say . . . Libby!" she exclaimed, with a sudden dawning of understanding. Her face broke into a grin. "Has some European man already proposed to you?"

"No," said Libby. "I hope he doesn't. I think I'm just a curiosity."

"Well, I should stick around in case he does. What fun! Couldn't I listen in on the proposal? It would make *such* a wonderful human interest story!" She caught sight of the horror on Libby's face, and laughed despite herself, shaking her head till her hair fell into her eyes. "Okay, no. But you'll have to remember every word he says. I wonder if the Irish propose differently."

"He isn't Irish, in the first place," said Libby.

"Well, what is he? Is he Romanian, or something exotic?" Henry leaned forward, her elbows resting on her knees. "Is he *Russian*? I've been dying to go to Russia. This could be my chance. "

"How quickly you forget poor Cap!" Libby exclaimed.

"I see *you* haven't forgotten him," Henry shot back. She took a lipstick from the bureau in front of her and rimmed her mouth with rose pink, then blotted it with a tissue and fired the tissue into a nearby wastepaper basket, overhand. "I'll take that as a good omen."

A week later, Lord Warburton came to call—but he wasn't alone. Libby was relieved to hear it. He'd brought his solicitor, from London.

"What is a solicitor?" demanded Henry, shaking both men's hands vigorously, then stepping back to study them.

"It's a sort of a lawyer," said the solicitor, whose name was Roger Pye.

"And do you have a sort of law degree?" asked Henry. She'd whipped out her pencil and notebook.

"Yes," said Roger Pye mildly. He was a tall man, with stooped shoulders and a very long, aristocratic nose.

"How many sisters and brothers do you have?" Henry demanded.

"Two of each," he answered promptly. While he was naming them, Lord Warburton strolled behind and took a quick glance at Henry's notebook.

"Be careful, Pye," he said. "She's writing all this down. She's even got your ums and ahs in here. Libby, will you show me around the gardens, since your cousin is ill disposed today?"

"He caught an awful cold," she answered. "But there isn't much new to see since your last visit."

"Then it won't take long to see it," he said, striding toward the door. Libby looked helplessly at her friend, shrugging, then followed.

"Wait!" called Henry. "I have a dozen questions to ask you about being a lord!"

This only made Warburton move faster. "Later!" he called back over his shoulder.

Libby grabbed her jacket off a hook and hurried after him. Mr. Pye was laughing at something Henry had just said and clapping his hands in delight.

"This is better than a play!" he was saying. "Do go on."

"Have you many friends like her?" asked Lord Warburton when they were safely outside.

"There are not many people in the world as good as Henrietta Capone," answered Libby. There had been a frost earlier; the dark-red lilies had turned black, and those that hadn't fallen hung crumpled and soft-looking. "Not much to see," she pointed out needlessly.

"I didn't come to see the lilies, I came to see you," said Warburton. "To ask if you could take me seriously, if you would be my wife." The words tumbled out as if he wanted to get rid of them as quickly as possible.

"Your wife," said Libby in despair.

"That's right," he said, "but you needn't answer right away. We've only known each other a few months. I imagine it comes as something of a shock, a question like that. It's asking a lot of a person. I'm aware of that. I'm aware how little you know me. Only I just thought—you know—on the chance . . ."

Libby plucked a lily from its stem. "I'm . . . very grateful," she murmured. She stroked a few petals of the flower and watched it fall apart. "But I don't think I would suit you. I truly don't."

"No, don't say that," said Warburton. "Surely you want to take a little time to think things over. Perhaps I put the matter badly. I haven't anyone to advise me in these things."

"Not even your solicitor?" teased Libby, with a sad smile.

"Damn my solicitor!" he cried. "I couldn't shake him off; he wanted to meet some real live Americans. As if there aren't dozens of them wandering around London all hours of the night."

"I hope there aren't," Libby answered. "He seems like a kind man. . . . His eyes look sad even when his mouth smiles. Mr. Pye, is it?"

"Why in God's name are we talking about Pye?" Lord Warburton demanded.

"Because I've nothing good to say about us," said Libby. "About you and me—we've only just met. And your proposal makes me feel shy and uncomfortable, and you deserve better than I can give."

Lord Warburton sat down heavily on a stone bench. He was a large man, so when he sat heavily, it had the effect of a very large object giving in to the laws of gravity. And indeed, his expression was graver than Libby had ever seen it. But then he smiled, kindly. He patted the bench beside him, and when Libby hesitated, he patted it more firmly. "I won't bite," he said. "Sit down."

She sat. In her dark-gray wool jacket, her face looked pale and somber. She still held the flower in the palm of her hand, and now she touched the edges of its petals.

"Is it the Irish climate?" he said, glancing down at her hand. "I know it's cold and damp here. But we can live elsewhere, you know. We can go anywhere in the wide world that you like!"

He put his arms out as he spoke, and Libby could not help but feel the ardor of it—it was like an embrace, the warmth of his words, as sweet and keen as the fragrance of the lily she was now crumpling in her hand as her fist opened and closed. Her mother and father had only known each other a few weeks when they eloped—but that was another time, another age. And that marriage had been a disaster. She remembered her mother in tears behind a closed door. She wished she could feel differently about Lord Warburton. But she drew away as instinctively as a bird that finds itself in a vast cage. The bars were there, no matter how much she might try to ignore them.

"I don't think I want to be married," she said.

"Well . . . many women start out that way," he said, smiling slightly at his own joke.

She tossed the lily down to the ground and stood. She began pacing back and forth. Whether she knew it or not, she was wringing her hands. "I'm sorry—I can't. I mustn't and I can't!"

"Is there some rule against it? Do you have to wait a certain period before you become engaged? I hadn't thought of that. Your father was Jewish, wasn't he? Is it a religious prohibition? I can wait, you know—as long as you say."

"No, it isn't that!" Her eyes were wide. "I think I'm not going to marry at all. Ever. I don't have the patience for it."

"Are you bent on a life of misery and loneliness?"

"Of course not," she said. "I'm determined to be happy, I've always said so—ask anyone. But I can't live by turning away. By . . . separating myself."

"Separating yourself?" He looked startled and faintly amused. "Separating yourself from what?"

"From life! From my own fate. From the usual chances and dangers, what other people know and suffer."

"My dear Libby, I'm not the emperor of China!" he exclaimed. "I'm not offering you protection from every vicissitude—I wish I could. I'm just offering a comfortable sort of life together."

"But I distrust comfort," she said, standing at one end of the bench. She could not take her eyes from the blossom she had tossed down on the ground. Warburton looked at it too, but only glancingly.

"I could do my best to make you uncomfortable," he said, trying to smile.

"You're doing a fair job now." She tried to soften the blow. "I know you'll live to marry a far better woman than I."

"Please don't say that. It's not fair to either of us. I think you are the most beautiful soul I've ever met. I'm not easily touched," said Lord Warburton slowly, "and I can't explain it when I am. . . . But when I am touched, it's for life, Miss Archer. . . . It's for life."

She looked into his blue eyes. One eye was slightly different from the other in size and shape, which added to his look of shyness or evasiveness, but he was trying, she realized, to answer her gaze head-on, as best he could. She knew just enough to feel the loss. There was more to him, she realized, than she would ever deserve to know.

Chapter Eight

"I don't see why we have to run away," complained Henrietta. She was rolling up her clothing into neat little cylinders and stowing them in her one compact and elegant bag. Henrietta always traveled light.

"We aren't running," answered Libby. "We're just going." She stifled her guilt at not confiding more fully in her closest friend. But if she mentioned Warburton's proposal, Henry would have teased her to death with a hundred questions, and she wasn't ready for that, not yet.

Henry plunked down on the bed. "Then *why* are we going?" she demanded. "Why *now*?"

"Because my aunt misses her house in Rome."

"She ought to miss her home in America!"

"Perhaps you think she ought to," answered Libby evenly, "but she doesn't. And I am her guest—and so, for the moment, are you."

"I suppose you're saying I've not been a good one."

"Well, aside from taking snapshots of people when they don't like it, and scribbling down everything everybody says, and arguing with my aunt every time she opens her mouth—"

"Are you pretending this sudden flight has nothing to do with the fact that Cap Lockwood is flying over here? And the poor man will find you gone! I'm surprised at you, Libby. I never thought you were heartless."

"I am not heartless," said Libby. "Give me some time, however . . ."

"Why Paris, anyway? I thought your aunt lived in Rome."

"She wants to visit some shops first," said Libby. She held up two blouses to compare them and ended up putting both into her suitcase. "She thinks I should try the new telescope-shaped dress. My aunt has very definite ideas about fashion."

Henry moved to block Libby's path from closet to suitcase. "And you, Libby? What are your definite ideas?"

Libby gestured: she wore a boatneck striped T-shirt, short, fitted pants, and black sandals. "Mine apparently are hopelessly out of date."

"Will you really let that poor man fly across the ocean without even catching sight of you?"

Libby put her head in both her hands. "I didn't ask him to come."

"You didn't tell him *not* to."

"I *did*—in a manner of speaking."

"That was not the manner I ever saw."

"Are you trying to say I encouraged him?" The two friends looked at each other for a moment, without speaking. Libby dropped her gaze first. "I hardly know what I am doing when I am around that man," said Libby. She stood again, with a sudden renewal of energy. "And that is exactly why I can't be around him. . . . I don't trust myself."

Henry considered Libby's words over the next few hours, moving around Gardencourt as quietly as a cat, and then finally she sought out her young host. Henry had struggled with her conscience but her sense of justice, even of destiny, won out. She found Lazarus Sachs drooping in a lemon-yellow upholstered chair by a large window, gazing out at a broad expanse of lawn. She tapped a silver pen against her teeth.

"I cannot describe this shade of green," she said, glancing over his shoulder.

"No one said you had to," Lazarus replied. He tried to smile, but his eyes were weary.

"You look sick," said Henry bluntly.

"I *am* sick," he answered, pleasantly enough.

"I would like you to do me a great favor nonetheless," said Henry, sitting in a chair across from him. "Will you say yes?"

"Are you proposing to me?" asked Lazarus.

Henry cocked her head at him. She regarded him with one bright eye, much like a bird. "Why do you always talk about marriage?" she said. "It is not a topic that especially interests me."

"Won't you change your mind if I ask you to be mine?" said Lazarus.

Henry frowned. "That was rude. You have no intention of asking, and I have no intention of considering such a proposal. Do you harp on it to remind me that I am a woman, and alone? I know it very well. Nonetheless I have my own thoughts and feelings, and believe I am entitled to them."

Lazarus inclined his head. "Indeed," he said humbly. "Tell me the favor, and I will do it if it is within my poor power."

"It lies in your power to make sure that your cousin marries the right man," she answered. "And that she doesn't marry the wrong one."

Lazarus could not hide his surprise. "Has Warburton got you meddling on his behalf?"

"Who?" said Henry. "The tall English gentleman?"

"Never mind," said Lazarus. "Go on."

"Lord Warburton?" said Henry. "The one with the long legs? You think I want Libby to marry *him*?"

"He's a fine fellow," said Lazarus.

Henry jumped to her feet and paced, swiveling quickly each time she turned. She tugged at a strand of her own curly hair. "I was afraid of this!"

"You needn't be afraid," said Lazarus soothingly. "She's already turned him down."

Henry stopped in her tracks. Her cheeks were flushed. "Has she?" she exclaimed. "Then there is hope!" She went on as if speaking to herself. "Good! She's turned down British royalty. Think of that, Mr. Lockwood!"

"Who is Mr. Lockwood?" asked Lazarus, bewildered.

"He is a fine American man," said Henry, resuming her seat across from her host. "A businessman, a forward thinker, and an inventor."

"You ought to write his biography," Lazarus observed.

"Perhaps one day I will," retorted Henry. "He might make history someday. I could believe it."

"American history, you mean," said Lazarus, with a gleam in his formerly listless eye. He was never more himself and alive than when he was teasing.

"Is there anything wrong with American history?" Henrietta said doggedly.

"It has a few blotches on it," said Lazarus. "Like every place else."

"Name two," said Henry defiantly.

"Slavery, and the treatment of your native Indians," retorted Lazarus. He held up two fingers, then closed them into a fist and banged on his knee, a habit he had when worked up. "Nothing worse than most countries, Miss Capone. Humankind is a blighted race. We should be wiped off the face of the earth. My own adopted country, Ireland, has a history of senseless murder, going on for centuries. America at least was built on a few beautiful ideas."

"Spoken like a true patriot," Henry said warmly, but Lazarus glowered.

"Patriotism," he said. "Another vile notion. I think your Senator Joe McCarthy is considered a patriot, isn't he?"

She flushed. "My country has been in its own dark ages lately. It's not accidental that I've left just now." She tilted back the chair she sat in till it balanced precariously on its two rear legs, the top of the chair leaning against the wall. Lazarus could not tell her that it was a precious antique, nor that she was probably ruining the wallpaper, though both were true. He merely sat admiring her lovely profile as she sat ruminating. "But it never lasts, that's one comfort," she said. "Terrible though it may be. All tyrannies, all the worst moments in history, they don't go on forever. 'Have you no sense of decency, sir? At long last, have you left no sense of decency?'"

"A great many lives were destroyed before those words were spoken," noted Lazarus. "And others continue to be ruined."

"Yes, too many." He wondered if she knew how beautiful she looked when she smiled ruefully like that, with her lovely mouth pulling down, readying itself to frown. "Granted. I may have to remove the word *patriot* from my vocabulary."

"It would be no loss if you did," Lazarus answered. "And you would still have so many words left!"

"Yes," she said. "And so, may I say just a few on behalf of Mr. Lockwood?"

His eyes glinted. "I wish you would. I'm extremely interested."

"He is a man of ideas . . . of action. He is working on a host of interesting inventions at the moment. One of them has to do with improving phonographs. One has to do with computers—making them smaller, he says."

"That's an idea," said Lazarus, sitting up straighter. "People could have them right in their own homes."

"I'm glad you agree." She brought the chair back down on four legs, much to Lazarus's relief. "More to the point, he is head over heels in love with Libby and I believe she is in love with him, though she won't admit it. They belong together. You've never seen a homely man look more handsome than when he looks at her. She certainly encouraged him at one point, and it's not like her to go back on a promise. He has flown to Ireland to see what good it might do. I hope it will do some good. I am no romantic, as you've no doubt guessed, but those two people were made for each other. I am concerned for both their happiness—and he's come a long way to see her."

"Does my cousin know he's here?"

Henry glowered at him defiantly. "She does. But we are about to leave for Paris. To buy dresses with telescoped waists, and the proper heels. And she stands to lose her best chance at happiness."

"I see," said Lazarus.

"I'd like your permission to invite Mr. Lockwood here, to Gardencourt."

"You don't need my permission," he protested, waving her off with one hand.

"Nonetheless I'd like to have it."

"When?" he asked.

She took a breath. "We leave tomorrow. I'd like you to invite him to tea, or whatever you call it, today."

"Oh, Lord," he groaned. "You want to make me your accomplice. Libby will be furious at both of us." He turned his head sideways and stole a glance at her, stalling for time. "You honestly believe she's in love with him?"

"I do," she said.

"And you think he's worthy of her?"

"I'm sure of it," she said. "I've never met anyone like him. He would move heaven and earth for her—and I think he could do it too! He has the courage of ten other men."

"Are you sure you're not in love with him yourself?" asked Lazarus.

"Very sure," she said, without resentment. "I love him like a brother."

"That dooms him then."

"Maybe as far as I am concerned," she said. "However, I am not the one he's just flown thousands of miles to see."

"Can't we tell her? Have her invite him herself?"

Henry shook her head vehemently. "She'd run. Trust me, she would bolt. But she would be running away from the best part of herself—from her own happiness. She might not realize it now, but she'd know it someday, when it was too late. She seems to think she doesn't deserve to be happy. And I can't bear to sit idly by and watch that happen."

"I can't imagine you ever doing that, Miss Capone." Lazarus leaned forward and extended one long, thin arm. "All right," he said. "I'm in."

They shook on it.

Gardencourt was strangely empty, Libby observed. Her aunt had taken her uncle to see one of her own doctors—one of her quacks, he called it—a woman near Derry who practiced homeopathy. Mr. Pye had come to call on Henry and introduce her around to his friends, and Lazarus had simply—disappeared.

Already packed for the next day's travel abroad, Libby felt inside herself that curious vacancy that occurs before a journey. Gardencourt just now reminded her of her own Rochester house in mourning, after her father had died. All that was missing, she thought, was the black crepe looped around the doorknobs and the cards and sympathy notes of friends. She wandered aimlessly into the portrait gallery and found herself face-to-face with the painted young woman holding the dog. When she leaned in to study the brush strokes, a yapping sound seemed to come from the painting itself. Instead she looked down and laughed to see her cousin's small white dog stepping on her feet. She scooped him up and gazed into the painting as if into a mirror—unconsciously echoing the pose of the woman within.

Then she turned resolutely and set off for the library. Gardencourt had an impressive collection of books, and Libby had promised herself to read at least two books a week while in Ireland. Mr. Lockwood's scornful words about her reading habits still stung. She had not lived up to her own lofty ideals. She had thumbed to the middle of one or two volumes and never gotten any farther.

With renewed vigor—and a slight sense of futility, since she would be traveling with her aunt and Henry for the next month or two at least—she marched into the library, still carrying the small dog, and pulled out the heaviest, most serious-looking volume she could find. Something on Roman history.

She selected an apple out of a large gilded bowl in the center of the table. She sat down with the dog in her lap, pulled the heavy volume toward her, and began to read. The introduction was distressingly dense. She checked the back of the book—yes, it really was more than eight hundred pages long—and began again, this time at the first chapter, which gave her the pleasant sensation of already having made a good beginning. She crunched into the apple and was immediately distracted by the play of light at the windows. The side panes were made of leaded glass and cast bright oblongs of rainbows along the wooden table. She reached out and touched one rainbow, letting it alight on the end of her finger. She stood, grabbing both dog and apple, and abandoned the book in the middle of the table. She hoisted herself up onto the window seat, sitting directly in the late afternoon sunlight, angled sideways, free to admire both the library itself and the green view stretching outside. The dog curled up at her feet.

"I will never," she said softly to herself, "get used to all this green." Albany would be gold-and-red ombré by now, but early fall had not dimmed Ireland's palette. Roses still bloomed by the window—huge dark-pink roses, as big as her hand, and chrysanthemums climbed their stakes toward a blue sky streaked with opal clouds. Everywhere else as far as her eye could see were swaths of brilliant green reaching almost to the edge of the sea, dotted here and there with the distant white backs of sheep. Libby sat with her knees pulled up to her chest, and her arms around her knees.

Just then she heard muffled voices outside the door. One of them, the bass voice, made her leap from the window seat as if catapulted.

"Really, sir," protested the young maid outside, in a thick Irish brogue, ". . . must be announced. You'll lose both my job and head, at that. Thank you, sir, but there's no need to . . . but you're generous, sir."

It wasn't Margaret, Libby thought in a panic. Margaret would have protected her. Libby made one wild pull at the handle of the large picture window and gave up that escape route as impossible. Instead she grabbed the nearest volume off a library shelf at random, clutching it to her like a shield. She should have dressed more carefully. She wished, at least, that she had brushed and set her hair.

The maid was still protesting and thanking the man, and the man's voice broke in brusquely. "Will you let me get by?" There was a sharp rapping at the door. "Libby? Are you there?"

She didn't answer—she could not answer. The door flung open, with the young maid jabbering apologies and laughing explanations, but there he was, his face as hatched and dark as a dime-store Indian's, Caspar Lockwood striding across the room toward her while the little dog danced up and down along the window seat, barking madly.

"I always seem to find you in libraries," Cap said, looking around. "I didn't realize you were such a reader."

"How did you find me?" she demanded, when she could recover her voice.

"What do you mean?" He stopped a few feet short of her, though he'd been about to . . . do what? She wasn't sure, but felt as if she'd been saved, snatched from the jaws of some breathtaking danger. "I was invited here. Your cousin invited me."

"My cousin?" she said blankly. Her voice shook. She bit her lips as if that might keep her voice steady.

"A biblical name. Ezekiel? I've been waiting for some word. It didn't sound like a prank call. He didn't ask if my refrigerator was running."

"My cousin," Libby said again. "Lazarus."

"Invited me to tea, yes. Lazarus. Four o'clock." Cap checked his watch and tapped it with his forefinger. "I was prompt."

"You always are," she said in a faint voice.

"You make my virtues sound like faults," he said.

"Well, fair enough." She tried to smile. "You make my faults out to be virtues."

They stood there looking at each other. She had a tremendous desire to reach out and stroke his dark face, to watch his expression change. She thought his skin must feel very warm. No one else looked like him. The breathing silence between them, she realized, was far more dangerous than words. The little dog went on dancing and barking on the ledge. Libby went and got the dog, but he wriggled out of her arms and leaped onto the floor, running mad circles around Cap Lockwood's feet. Cap was wearing elegant brown wingtips, burnished like old wood. Her eyes were riveted on his shoes. Had she even said hello? The dog went on barking madly.

"I'm sorry," she said. "This dog is lovely but very badly behaved. He's never had any training and won't obey."

"Sit," said Cap to the dog. The dog immediately sat. "Down," said Cap. The little dog lay down, panting.

"No one told me you were coming today," she said. "Henrietta is behind this. It . . . wasn't kind."

"She means well," Cap said mildly.

"Good intentions—" She stopped. "I can't pretend I'm not glad to see your face. I'm very glad . . . I'm very glad indeed to see you."

He crossed toward her, came very close, and then stopped still. She shivered. He took her hand between both of his, shook the hand, in a manner of speaking—it was half a handshake and half a caress—then let go and stepped back. The silences between them, as they had always been, were long and electric. Libby resisted the impulse to begin babbling. He stood shifting his weight from one long leg to the other, looking around the room. "I'm here," he said in a voice that restored normality. "I've come a long way. May I sit down?"

"Of course. Please do," she said. She stood beside the long library table and gestured at a seat across. He sat. She remained standing. "Can I get you some tea?" she asked. "Are you hungry? Shall I ring for something?"

He shook his head, and a few lank pieces of dark hair dropped in front of his eyes. She remembered this. Her hand moved in the air as if to brush them back, but did no such thing. "Are you interested in raising birds now?" he asked.

"What?" she said blankly.

He gestured toward the big book she clutched. "*Raising the Home Duck Flock*," he said.

"Oh!" She flushed. "Not really." She set the terrible book on the table, face down. Why, of all possible volumes, this one? She sat catty-corner to him, pushing the book back and forth, back and forth.

"I flew to Ireland to see if you were well," Cap said. He held up a hand. "I know you sent a card, but I needed to see for myself. A post-card reveals nothing. I wondered if you were homesick. If you wanted to come home, and perhaps might have felt"—he hesitated, searching for the right words—"that you didn't have a place to come home to. I wanted to say clearly that you always have a place. As long as I'm alive, Libby, and even after I'm gone, you will always have a place with me."

Her eyes shone at him. They were very green and bright just now. She seemed like some exotic creature, perhaps some woodland animal. One misstep and she might turn and bolt.

"That is so kind," she said. Her voice quavered. She had not stopped shivering—around him her body often reacted this way, and she hated it.

"I don't say it to be kind," he told her.

"Which only makes it kinder."

"Or more stupid. . . . The last time I saw you, you told me never to come near you."

"I don't remember saying never," she said.

"To go away for ten years, or a hundred years—it's all the same."

"I disagree. If you could just stop thinking of me . . . a certain way . . . for even a few months, I'm sure we could be friends again."

"That is just what I don't want. Is it your plan," he said speaking slowly and carefully, "that if I begin not thinking about you for a certain fixed period of time, I might find that I could keep it up indefinitely?"

She pulled *Raising the Home Duck Flock* toward her, then pushed it away again. Why, at least, couldn't she have been holding the first book? The Roman history. "Indefinitely is more than I'd ask. More than I'd want, even."

"I won't stop thinking about you," he said bluntly. "My thoughts are my own, Libby. You can't control them. And you can't stop my loving you."

"You might try," she insisted.

"My efforts too are my own," he said. "If you are a strong person, you can't help loving strongly. Loving ardently. That's simply my nature. Don't try to change me."

"No," she said. "I have no right to do that." She looked down and there were his shoes again; his impossibly beautiful, masculine leather shoes. Her cousin's white dog lay right by the shoes, wagging his tail as if in admiration or delight. "Think of me or not," she said, "but please let me be for a year or two. I am happy here. I am finding my way."

His firm lips tightened. "Which do you want? There's all the difference in the world between one year and two."

"Call it two then."

He flushed as if she had slapped him. Yet of all the people she might ever wish to hurt, he was the very last. He had been kind when she was at her lowest point. He'd made her think her captivity, the narrowness of her life in Rochester, might not last forever. He put one hand down and automatically, hypnotically stroked the dog from head to flank. "And what's to be my reward for all this patience?" he asked.

"You'll have my gratitude and admiration," she said. "I hope that's worth something."

He did not return her smile. "I don't give a fig for your admiration, Libby," he said. "When will you marry me? That's all I care about."

"Are we back to that again so soon?" she exclaimed impatiently. "I don't want to marry you or anyone else, and it's no kindness to me if you insist. Listen, Cap . . . isn't it possible you don't have the right to change me, either? Perhaps I will never want to marry . . ." She saw his look and colored. "Yes, never! It's how I feel right now, and I have as much right to my thoughts and feelings as you have to yours. Do men have all the say in the matter? Why not a woman? She must always be chosen—she herself can never choose."

"I want you to choose me," Cap said grimly. "I'd settle for nothing less."

"Then I choose you for my friend. Listen, Cap," she pleaded. "I know women say they want to be friends when they want nothing at all, but if you let a little time pass, we might become real friends again, as we once were. Do you remember our long walks together? . . . How we would drive beside the lake with the windows rolled down?"

"I remember," he said. "You walked barefoot on the boardwalk at Charlotte Beach one night. In a yellow two-piece bathing suit." He had come up behind her and put his arms around her waist that night. But neither of them mentioned that part.

"Give me my chance," she pleaded. "Let me see all I can. A woman has so little freedom in her life. My chance has come unexpectedly, and at great cost. You of all people know it, Cap. You knew me in my father's house. When was I free to breathe my own air? To think my own thoughts, even? You have always been free to do as you like."

"Yes, except where it matters most," he said. He got up and pushed back his chair. The little dog jumped to its feet as well. "I will leave you alone," he said. "I'll fly back to America tomorrow." He paused at the door, turning to look at her. "Only—I hate to lose sight of you."

"I won't do anything that will make you ashamed of me," she promised.

"You'll marry someone else, as sure as I'm standing here," he said.

"Do you think I'm so easily won?" she shot back. "I've already turned down a British lord." She couldn't keep the note of bragging out of her voice.

"Have you?" he said. But he put his hand on the doorknob. "I suppose you expect me to be happy. I'm not. I'm glad he's disappointed. But it only means you are preparing for some grander gesture. A lord would never do for you—oh no! It must be a pauper, I suppose . . . or a thief. Someone for you to rescue!"

"Won't you at least stay for tea?" she asked. "Must you always slam in and out with a parting shot?"

"No. I won't stay," he said.

"Can't you be friendly?" she begged.

"I'm not a friendly man," he replied. "I'm barely civil. You've told me so yourself, a hundred times. Give Henry my regards. Tell her I'll see her back in New York." He pulled the doorknob back and forth. "Just watch out for dazzling men, Libby. Especially the clever ones. Try not to fall too hard for the worst of them."

She rose but made no move to follow him out. "Why would I," she said, "when I couldn't fall for the best of them?"

He pulled the door open and looked into the hall. Something about it seemed to fill him with despair. His shoulders slumped. He looked, for almost the first time in their entire acquaintance, weary. "Explain to me how it's done, Libby. Tell me how to live alone for the next two years," he said.

"Oh, *you* should marry!" she exclaimed without thinking.

"God forgive you!" he muttered between clenched teeth, and stalked out.

Chapter Nine

Libby walked alone on a rainy autumn evening in Paris and was not surprised to hear silvery piano music pouring from her aunt's apartment window. It seemed as if it should always be raining in Paris, and as if music—she thought she recognized the composer, but couldn't be absolutely sure—should always be playing in a nearby room, at a slight distance.

She stopped and let the music drift over her with the soft rain. She had a rain bonnet in her coat pocket, but how could one wear something so hideous as a plastic rain bonnet in a place as beautiful as a Parisian street in the 5th arrondissement? Every chance she had, she wandered across one of the bridges and lost herself in the smallest winding streets of the Left Bank, as if trying to reach a point at which the street itself, and she herself in it, would disappear. It was the rare moment of quiet in this vast, ancient capital city that she loved most . . . the way the Parisian sky turned a shimmering shade of dark blue just before nightfall. She carried a bag of pastries in one hand and a baguette tucked under the other arm. Perhaps she was a cliché, but she didn't mind being a cliché just then. She stood in the street a moment, captivated, looking up. There was a stranger sitting framed in her aunt's bay window playing the piano: a woman whose profile was as perfect as a finely cut cameo, with golden hair piled neatly and tightly into a bun, a woman wearing a masculine-looking black suit. *How like Paris,* thought Libby, *to admit a stranger into her aunt's apartment, a stranger who played the piano so beautifully.*

She opened the front door and went up the stairs as quietly as possible, trying to step over the one riser that creaked, but even while she was easing the door open the woman swung around in one fluid movement and said in a soft, accentless voice, "I hope I haven't disturbed you?"

"Not at all," said Libby, crossing the room to shake the woman's hand. "I assume you are a friend of my aunt's. You play exquisitely. I thought at first it was a record album."

"Chopin," said the other woman, smiling and shrugging as if to suggest that Chopin must get all the credit, that his beautiful music played itself, and that she had nothing whatsoever to do with it. "I am Madame Merle," she added, rising from the piano. "But please—call me Clara."

"I'm Libby," she said, feeling self-conscious and ungainly, shaking the water off her bright-colored raincoat, which suddenly looked garish rather than chic, removing her damp things and looking awkwardly around for a place to put the baked goods. Madame Merle—the wonderful Clara—took them from her and immediately arranged everything to the best possible advantage.

"I know who you are," said the woman. "Your aunt is so happy to have your company."

"I am very grateful to my aunt," said Libby. "I never would have left my own country without her kind invitation. I am seeing and hearing," she said, gesturing toward the piano, a small but very good Boisselot & Fils, "so much. It's like a whole college education, being here in Europe."

"Oh, my dear," laughed the older woman. "It's a great deal more valuable than a college education."

Libby pushed her bangs out of her eyes. She tried glancing into the small mirror by the door. Did she really look as rumpled and chaotic as she felt, next to this poised blonde woman? "And did *you* go to college?" she asked eagerly.

The other woman's smile faded a shade. "I have taken night classes," she said. "But let us not talk about me. I am a dull subject. Tell me your first impressions of Europe—of Paris. It is your first visit, isn't it? It's been such a long time since I've looked at any place through fresh eyes."

"Have you met my friend Henrietta?" asked Libby. "She could describe everything much better than I. She is a professional writer," she added proudly.

"No, luckily there was no one at home but your aunt when I arrived," said Clara, with a crooked smile. "And your aunt has gone out. She gave me leave to sit and play. I seldom get to play on such a beautiful instrument. I hope you don't mind."

"I think I could just sit here and look at you all night!" Libby burst out. She didn't usually give way to her enthusiasms, but it was in her nature now and again to be carried away. And where would one be carried away, if not in Paris at dusk?

"How sweet of you!" returned Madame Merle. "Americans do say the funniest things. It's very charming. No wonder the rest of the world loves you."

"And where are you from?" asked Libby, failing to detect any clue.

"Oh, me—" Clara Merle laughed a tinkling laugh, a sound with silvery tones in it, but an undercurrent of sadness too. *Laughter like that is like music,* Libby thought. "I am from here . . . there . . . everywhere, I suppose. But chiefly I must say nowhere."

"And where did you get that wonderful suit?" Libby asked.

Clara sank into a small armchair just across from Libby, crossing her long slim legs and looking at them admiringly—as if the legs and the suit did not in fact belong to her. "Now that I can answer!" she said. "It is Chanel."

"A real Chanel?" asked Libby.

"Of course it is real!" A flash of annoyance came across Clara Merle's composed face, and two pinkish red spots appeared, one on each sculpted cheek. But her expression softened when she saw how she had flustered her new acquaintance.

"However, you mean no harm," said Clara. And then, as if speaking to herself, with a light laugh, "And really, what harm can she possibly do me?" Her whole look brightened; she appeared in that instant fifteen years younger. "You must forgive me, *chérie*. I live amongst people who say nothing by accident, who often wish to inflict harm. I have kept my guard up so long that I no longer remember how it works to let it down." She stood, removed the black jacket, and handed it to Libby.

"I could show you several ways to recognize the authentic from the frauds; for example, in the straightness of the seams, and the turn of the hand-sewn hem—and one must never trust the label. Never a label! They are so easily added on. . . . In fact, I, myself—but, never mind. Here. Try it on."

She helped Libby into the jacket and smoothed it over her shoulders, giving it an expert tug in the back. "Just so! It's all in the details, you know." She stepped back to take a look. "Very nice. Of course I am taller than you are, and a bit . . . fuller. But yes. Black becomes you. Look in the glass." And she steered Libby to a mirror, wherein both women were reflected. Madame Merle cocked her golden head, and stepped back a little, as if automatically.

"I have only recently given up wearing black," said Libby, looking not at herself but at the glamorous Madame Merle. She looked a bit like an older Grace Kelly. But she had other qualities that Grace Kelly would not have wanted to possess. A hardness. And two sharp lines around her lovely mouth, one on each side.

"Yes, I know," said Madame Merle. "Your aunt told me. I am so sorry for your loss."

"He was a drunk," blurted Libby. "I loved him very much. He was unhappy." She turned away from the mirror and removed the Chanel jacket, handing it back. "This is beautiful," she said. "But it doesn't really suit me."

"I agree." Clara nodded approvingly. "It's important to know what looks right on us and what doesn't. Sometimes I think that is the only choice we women have in this life. But then, you young women may change all that, in the future. A suit is like a coat of armor. Someday you may suddenly find you need one." She went to a small bag sitting by an armchair and fished out a pack of cigarettes. "Do you mind if I smoke?"

Libby shook her head.

"Don't begin, and you won't have to quit. One day we'll probably learn that cigarettes are deadly. But till then"—she lit the cigarette and breathed in deeply, tilting back her head—"I find it soothes me. Just as the ads say." She eyed Libby through a veil of smoke. It obscured her features. "It would be nice to have a friend, not for usefulness, but . . . simply, because." She smiled. "So tell me. Why are you here? First in Ireland with your decrepit uncle and cousin, and now in Europe with your aunt? Why are you here, really?" She spied an ashtray across the room and set it on top of the piano. "You can confide in me if you like. I know how to keep secrets."

"They are not decrepit," said Libby, feeling a trifle uneasy around this fascinating woman. "I'm only sorry that my uncle is ill."

"He is not as close to dying as your cousin," said Madame Merle. Then, expertly reading Libby's expression, she added, "I am very fond of Lazarus. Truly. And I know there are things one is not supposed to say—"

"Oh, but those are often the most important things!" Libby burst out. "You ask why I'm here. Just look." She pointed out the window, at the city of Paris, glimmering blue and gold outside the glass, and partly reflected within. "Look at this magnificent old city. It's all a dream—a childhood dream. To see the world! To really look at things, for myself, by myself. I could never have imagined it possible. . . . I am sorry, truly sorry, that my father's death led me here—but how can I not be grateful, all the same? I am in Paris, talking to you, a beautiful, accomplished woman wearing a real Chanel suit!"

Both women laughed, though for different reasons.

"I'm sorry to babble," said Libby, "but most girls I know will come to Paris for one reason only, on a continental tour of two weeks, to be shown a few ancient sites in their guidebook!"

"Ah yes," said Clara Merle, flicking ash from her cigarette. "I see them clutching their Baedekers to their breasts and scurrying after their mamas and papas."

"Or possibly on a honeymoon," added Libby. "Though Niagara Falls is more likely, or Miami Beach or California, and Paris only if the husband chooses, and only as he chooses. Do you know?" she went on. "In my high school class, three quarters of the girls are already married or engaged. I'm looked on almost as a criminal for not joining the ranks. And those few who have evaded marriage are told their choices are to be a teacher, a nurse, or a secretary. How many times have I heard those three professions trotted out! As if they were the only occupations on earth."

"I suppose there's always clerking in a store," said Clara. "I've done that myself, long ago. Selling perfume. Heavens! A lifetime ago."

"Yes, or a waitress, if you are from the lower classes. I think maybe the women in the lower classes do have more choices."

Clara Merle's eyes gleamed even through the smoke. "People from the middle and upper classes always think so," she said. "But the only real choice, you know—"

"Is whom a woman marries," Libby finished for her.

The two women looked at each other with genuine understanding.

"Exactly so," said Clara Merle. "And I am living proof that one cannot choose too carefully."

"Your husband—"

Clara shook her head.

"I'm so sorry," said Libby warmly.

"Don't be," said Clara. "It all happened a long time ago. Many lifetimes ago." She gazed out the window, onto the lights below. "It *is* incredibly beautiful, isn't it? Paris, in all its glory. Yet I prefer Rome." She took a drag from her cigarette. "At least I think I do, still. . . . You make me wonder about myself, if I even have a self anymore, and that's something I haven't done for a long while."

Libby studied her new friend, the soft features outlined blurrily against the dark window and the Parisian evening. After a quiet moment she said, "I'm afraid you have sometimes suffered a great deal."

Clara Merle turned her head slowly, lazily. "To have sometimes suffered—there's nothing original in that!"

"Yes, but some people give the impression of never having felt anything at all."

Clara flicked a long ash into the tray beside her. "There are more iron pots than porcelain, I suppose," she admitted. "But if you look closely enough, every one of us is crazed and chipped somewhere. No one is seamless. And the more seamless they appear, the more deeply they are likely to be scarred. Take it from me! I do very nicely, for instance, as long as I'm in the cool depths of the cupboard—surrounded by Joy perfume and some masking spices. But take me out into the full light of day—oh then, my dear, I'm a horror!"

"I'm sure that's not true!" protested Libby.

"I hope you'll go on believing it as long as possible. It makes a soothing change," said Clara. "But I could tell you tales . . ."

"I wish you would!" Libby exclaimed. "I love stories."

Clara regarded her appraisingly. "Perhaps one day I will," she said, stubbing out her cigarette. "It's not that I'm afraid you'll tell anyone else," she added. "We don't travel in the same circles. We don't even live in the same country! All the same, I'd like to keep our friendship for a while"

"I have friends I've known since childhood," said Libby.

"Yes, but you are at a cruel age," said Clara Merle. "You might judge me harshly in the end."

"I hope I am a fair judge," said Libby, a bit primly.

"I'm sure you are," laughed Clara. "Why would I be afraid of a poor one?"

Just then the front doorbell tinkled with its distinctive French tones, and Mrs. Sachs entered in her black winter furs, bringing a scent of winter and carrying parcels and bags, of which Libby and Clara immediately relieved her.

"I'm glad you two have met," said Mrs. Sachs. "That spares my having to make the introductions. I couldn't have planned it better. Where's Henrietta, not here? Good. Clara, what do you think of my new niece?"

"Hardly new!" protested Libby, blushing, but she was struggling not to seem overly interested in the answer.

"She's perfectly lovely," declared Madame Merle. "You couldn't have done better had you grown her from seed." All the women smiled at this joke.

"Madame Merle knows everything there is to know about the world," Mrs. Sachs announced, a note of pride in her voice.

"Ah, there isn't all that much to know," said Clara Merle. "And I only know very well the surface of things. The thin topmost layer."

"But that you know very well. You understand the forms," said Mrs. Sachs approvingly. "There is a great deal you could teach Libby."

"Well, I undertook my studies at an early age," laughed Clara lightly. "You might not think so, but I positively memorized all the books of etiquette, cover to cover. Where to put the oyster fork, when to wear short gloves, when to wear longer gloves. I studied those books as if my life depended on it."

"Clara Merle has exquisite manners," said Mrs. Sachs. "She could write a book herself."

"But there is nothing exquisite in being a writer," said Clara smoothly, "or indeed in being any sort of an artist. Only in being, oneself, a work of art."

"I think you are as magnificent as the Winged Victory!" exclaimed Libby.

The two older women exchanged tolerant glances.

"She certainly is an enthusiast," observed Mrs. Sachs drily.

"And unlike the Winged Victory, I have so far managed to keep my head," added Clara Merle, touching lightly her golden hair.

❧

Later that night the phone rang in the depths of the Paris apartment. Libby, sleeping in a single bed across from Henrietta, woke disoriented, her hand groping for the phone that lay several rooms away. Henry slept on, oblivious. Henry kept early hours, but when she was asleep nothing could rouse her.

Libby thought she heard a sound of dismay from her aunt, and then worried, murmured conversation down the hall. "Henry?" she said into the darkness. There was no reply. "I'm going to see what's going on."

She made her way into the sitting room, where Madame Merle and Mrs. Sachs were engaged in a whispered conversation. They stopped short at the sight of Libby, standing in her long navy robe, with white piping.

"Is it—" she asked. She was thinking of Lazarus, her voice trembling.

"It's my husband," said Mrs. Sachs. "He has taken a bad turn. We'll leave Paris first thing in the morning. Clara has kindly offered to come with us."

Clara Merle curved a reassuring arm around her elderly friend. "I'll call the airport and make the arrangements," she said. "You must try not to worry," she said to no one in particular.

"I worry most about Lazarus," said Mrs. Sachs simply.

"Help your aunt to pack," instructed Clara Merle. She was one of those women at her best in an emergency. "I'll make the plane reservations and arrange for a cab. We'll take the earliest flight available."

"Yes," said Mrs. Sachs. "All right. Thank you." She made a move to rise, but then her legs gave out from underneath her, and she sat down with a small cry of surprise. "We never expect this moment to come," she said. "I don't know why. It always does."

Madame Merle kept her arm around Mrs. Sachs. She gazed into the older woman's face as if looking for something, and failing to find it, bit her lip.

"I hope I've been a good enough wife," said Mrs. Sachs in a small dry voice.

Madame Merle stroked her friend's arm mechanically. "Ah, my dear. There is no book of rules to tell us how to do that."

Almost before they knew it, the women were back at Gardencourt, with no notion of how they had arrived, or how much time it had taken to get there. Everything seemed blurry, including the Irish landscape. It was drizzling lightly, as usual. Henrietta had been escorted off to Manchester, England, to spend time with Mr. Pye's helpful relatives and friends.

"I'll only be in the way, at a time like this," Henry told Libby.

"But you've only just met Mr. Pye!" Libby protested. "Don't be silly. Stay with us."

"I'm not being silly, I'm being sensible," said Henrietta. "Things are likely to get worse before they get better. Don't worry," she added. "I'll be back before you notice I'm gone. And I can return at a moment's notice. Take good care of your aunt. She's more fragile than she seems," said Henrietta, "and I don't trust that polished French friend of hers."

"Madame Merle is a compatriot of ours, as it turns out," said Libby, trying to smile.

"Well, she's not like any American *I've* ever met," Henry insisted. "She seems foreign through and through."

❧

Lazarus spent every spare moment in close quarters with his father, sleeping on a cot in the old man's room, taking meals at his father's bedside, so Libby barely saw him for the first days after their hurried arrival home to Ireland. It was just past eleven on the third night—she had been lying in bed, listening to the chiming of a grandfather's clock—when she heard a light tapping at her door. She assumed it to be her aunt.

"Come in," she called, sitting up in bed.

It was Lazarus who leaned at the door, wan and smiling, and covered in embarrassment upon finding his cousin in bed in her white nightgown. He looked at everything in the room but her, and nervously shuffled a deck of cards he plucked from his jacket pocket.

"Of course, it's late," he said. "I wasn't thinking." He spoke to a far corner of the wall, almost the ceiling.

"Would you hand me my robe?" she asked, and when he did, she put it on, tying the belt in a knot, slipped out of bed and hugged him tenderly.

"I'm sorry," he said. "I've been ignoring you terribly."

"I don't mind," she said eagerly, as if she'd been waiting for this excuse to say it. "Of course I don't mind. How is your father doing?"

Lazarus shrugged hopelessly. He walked around her room. He picked up objects, turning them around in his hands, and then setting them down again. It was a nervous habit with him. At the moment he was holding Libby's tortoise shell hairbrush. Then he startled, as if seeing it for the first time, and set it down hastily.

"I haven't seen you since you left for Paris," he said.

"A bit before. You disappeared suddenly—leaving me alone with an uninvited and unexpected guest."

"You still haven't forgiven me," said her cousin, "for inviting that American man here."

Libby turned her dark eyes upon him. They looked almost black in the low light, and scintillating. "It wasn't kind," she answered soberly. "I was . . . taken by surprise. I didn't think you would play me such a trick."

"I'm sorry," Lazarus said. He kicked one scuffed heel against the toe of the other worn slipper, staring down. "I won't try to make excuses for myself. Is he so terrible, this clever American inventor?"

"Tormentor, more like," she said.

He looked up at her. "If I had known that, I never would have allowed it!"

"Oh," she said with a small smile. "I am joking. Mostly joking. And I can't hold a grudge now . . . now—"

"Now that my father is dying?" Lazarus tried to speak matter-of-factly, but his voice broke on the last word.

Libby laid her hand over his and held it tightly. "I hope it won't be so," she said. "I hope you are wrong."

Lazarus looked away but left his hand in hers. "So do I," he said, "but when did hoping ever change a thing?" She read his long, dreary history in his drawn face and could make no reply. So she wisely said nothing. "His doctor's name is Dr. Hope," he added. "Ironically. But tell me about Paris," he went on, forcing animation into his voice. "Is it as glorious as ever? Did you stroll along the Champs-Élysées at dusk? Did you wander back and forth across the bridges?"

"I did." She smiled.

"And did you take a tour of L'Opéra, as I instructed?"

"I did indeed."

"Good, very good." He released her hand at last and threw himself into a chair nearby, stretching his long legs in front of him. "Tell me," he said, closing his eyes like a small boy getting ready to sleep. "What was the most marvelous thing you saw in all of Paris?"

"Oh, the most marvelous thing," she breathed. "That's easy. It was a woman, a friend of your mother's. It was Madame Merle."

His eyes flashed open. He was frowning. "Lucretia Merle?" he asked.

"She calls herself Clara. Is her name really Lucretia?"

"It suits her," he said. "I wouldn't be surprised if she wore a ring that contained a special poison for her enemies."

"She has enemies?" Libby exclaimed.

His lips turned in a downward smile. "My dear cousin," he said, "how could such a creature *not* have enemies? A good many more enemies than friends by now, I'd wager."

"I don't believe you," Libby said primly. "Perhaps people just don't appreciate her."

"I don't think a lack of appreciation has ever been her problem."

"A lack of understanding then," said Libby stubbornly. She refused to look her cousin in the face—she mustn't pick a fight with him now. She moved restlessly around the room, as he had done a few minutes earlier, picking up a small ivory figurine and putting it back down again unseen.

"That may be so," he said, watching her pace. "It is hard to understand someone so deep."

"We agree on that, at least!" she said with a toss of her head.

"There are depths and there are depths," said Lazarus.

"You are trying to say something without saying it." Libby fiddled with a pair of candlesticks, turning them round and round in her strong, slim fingers. Then she set them down with a light thunk. "You may as well tell me her flaws," she said. "I can see you're dying to."

"That is exactly the problem," Lazarus said. "Madame Merle has no flaws."

"Oh, you think everyone is perfect!" she exclaimed.

"Not so," said Lazarus.

"You described Lord Warburton as a perfect specimen," she said. "And you called Henrietta the perfect word chaser one day," she added, "and she sulked in her room for an hour."

"Henrietta understands me," he said.

"But she doesn't approve of you."

"That is *because* she understands me," said Lazarus.

"And I imagine you think I am perfect too, in some way."

"I do not," he said more soberly. "I think you are marvelous—you know I do—but far from perfect. It's exactly your imperfections that interest me most. You are still in the process of becoming, but Madame Merle is a finished product. She is . . . manufactured. In everyone else on earth one can find a weakness, some touch of humanity, but Madame Merle has no flaw, not the tiniest crack. There is no way in. She's as smooth as an egg." He thought for a moment and added, "She wears too much hairspray. Have you noticed? Her head looks like a polished helmet."

"I have been known to use hairspray myself. It's not like you to be so trivial."

"I don't like the way she smells."

"Lazarus!" chided Libby.

"There is nothing trivial about the way someone smells," said Lazarus. "It carries their whole essence. She smells of chemicals and perfume."

"I suppose you're trying to say she's too worldly," said Libby.

"Too worldly?" He threw his arms out. "She is the whole wide civilized world itself."

"You were in love with her, and she let you down!" Libby cried. "That's it. You're turning color. I'm right, aren't I?"

"How can I have been? She was married to Monsieur Merle when we met."

"Did he die?"

"So she says. Any husband of Madame Merle would be likely to die."

"How unpleasantly you say that!" exclaimed Libby. "I think you were in love with her."

Lazarus moved to sit on the end of Libby's bed and looked at her earnestly. "You may think what you like," he said, "but there is more than one way to be let down by a woman. You may believe they are real—that they are trustworthy."

"Has she any children?" asked Libby.

"No, thank God!"

"Thank God?" Libby echoed.

"She would be likely to spoil them."

"Unlike *your* father," said Libby with a smile.

"You have a point," said Lazarus. "And that reminds me I must go back to him. He sleeps a good deal of the time, but when he opens his eyes, I want him always to see me there."

"You've deserved your spoiling," said Libby gently.

"I only want you to"—Lazarus leaned forward, his fists digging into his thin legs—"I want you to be safe," he said. "That's why I'm warning you off Lucretia Merle."

"Clara," Libby corrected him.

"Clara, Lucretia—"

"But, my sweet cousin," she said, "none of us is safe. Haven't you learned that even yet?"

Mr. Sachs baffled the doctors with the violence of his recoveries and failures. He was as mercurial in illness as he'd been in health, and his capacity for rebounding appeared limitless. One day he could seem close to the very end, with night nurses hovering over him and Mrs. Sachs studiously avoiding him, and a day later he'd be not merely sitting up in bed, but carrying on raucous conversations with his son and flirting with the nurses.

Libby came to see him at intervals. She had never really known what to say to a truly sick person, believing she had been a poor nurse for her own father. Libby had a terrible, secret fear that she had made matters worse. She carried that worry into the present. Once, as she sat beside her uncle, he slept so quietly that she thought he had died on her watch, and she felt a terror and an excitement that were equally unacceptable to her sense of herself. If anything could have damaged Libby's own high regard for herself, it would have been at moments like this, when she viewed herself and her weaknesses all too clearly.

Her uncle's gaze was always gentle, yet she felt him watching her keenly—looking for signs of she didn't know quite what. He had dark-brown eyes, and they were clever and kind, studying her. She brought in trays of tea and biscuits, and issues of *LIFE* and *Look* magazine, and she amused him with some of the women's magazines she liked best—*McCall's*, *Woman's Own*. The articles, which she studied in secret with a certain degree of interest, made him roar with laughter.

"And is a wife always supposed to greet her husband with a smile at the door?" he asked incredulously. "Is that how they do it these days? What if the pipes break? What if there's been an earthquake—still 'with her lipstick and heels on, and a welcoming smile?' Apparently no one told *my* wife any of that," he mused. "I knew we were doing something wrong." He put one thin hand on the magazine, which forced Libby to look up again, to meet those bright eyes of his. "Forgive me if I'm nosy." He cleared his throat. "I heard you turned Lord Warburton down. Is it because you were afraid you wouldn't always be grinning at him?"

"I was afraid we wouldn't suit. Do you think I did wrong, Uncle?" she asked.

He had shut his eyes and he was smiling, patting the magazine page as if it were her hand. "No," he said. "No . . . I think you did just right."

Libby provided her best service for her uncle without ever recognizing she was doing it. She gave him something to consider. She gave him something like hope, almost amounting to a plan. But none of this would he have ever discussed with her directly. Instead he talked to his son, Lazarus, about it, close to the end.

The old man was having a good week, though he felt an increasing tiredness, like someone sinking toward sleep. He had not had the energy even to sit upright. He simply lay on his back and drifted. It was not an altogether unpleasant sensation—neither was it altogether pleasant. *Dying,* he thought, *might be just a matter of exhaustion in the end.*

When he mentioned this to his son, Lazarus said, "Oh, we'll have you sitting up again soon."

"Not unless you intend to bury me upright, like one of the Pharaohs," said his father.

"Oh no," argued Lazarus. "You'll soon be well again."

"It's not so bad," said his father, touching his son's long, thin arm where it lay near him on the bed. "But we have never lied to each other. Why should we do so now, at the end? I'd like to talk to you about what's really on my mind."

"Won't it tire you?" asked Lazarus.

"Doesn't matter. I'll soon have all the rest I need." The old man moved his head on the pillow to see his son better. "I want to talk about you."

Lazarus shuffled his pack of cards. He poured them from one hand to the other. "Can't we pick a brighter topic?"

"I've always been proud of how bright you are," said Mr. Sachs. "I wanted so much to see you truly happy. Happy and in your own element. I don't mind anything, really, except leaving you without first seeing that."

"If you leave, I won't do anything but miss you," said Lazarus.

"That's what I'm afraid of. That's what I want to talk about." He moved his eyes to a crystal water glass with a straw sticking out of it, and Lazarus, understanding at once, brought it to his father's lips and held it while his father drank. His father nodded and released the straw when he was done. "You will need something new."

"You mean like a hobby? I have many." Lazarus shuffled the cards again, to demonstrate.

"No. I have been a placeholder for you too long. I mean something real. . . . What about marriage?"

"What about it?"

Mr. Sachs barely smiled. "What about . . . your cousin Libby? She's no blood relation, you know."

"What about her?" Lazarus held his face very still.

"You'll be very well off," said the father. "You'll be a wealthy man."

"We talked about money a year ago," said Lazarus. "You know I don't want much. There are far better causes than mine."

Then the old man did smile, thinly. "Yes, I remember. We've made some charities happy. And I've left your mother the portion a good wife should get—just as if she'd actually been a good wife. But you'll still have more than enough for one—plenty for two."

"That's more than ample then. I'm only one."

"It's not good to live alone. I've been alone too much, and I am married. I don't want you to think that it's always like this, a marriage. I've probably failed you there. Setting a poor example all these years."

"You have in no way failed me," said Lazarus.

"What do you think of your cousin?"

"Do you mean . . . as a person?"

Mr. Sachs raised one hand and let it drop back down onto the bed. "I mean as a wife."

Lazarus scooted his own chair in closer. "Dearest Daddy." He was silent a minute, struggling for what tone to take. "Are you proposing that I should buy Libby as a bride? I don't think she's for sale."

"Are you in love with her?"

Lazarus did not answer. He kept his head down, studying the floor.

"She's very fond of you, you know," the old man went on. His voice sounded querulous, as if he'd been having an ongoing argument with himself over this. "She turned down Lord Warburton. I think that's a good sign."

"It may be a sign that she doesn't wish to marry Lord Warburton. It may mean she doesn't want to marry anyone at all. She turned down some suitor from America as well. Someone she's known a long time. An industrialist."

"Even better," said the father. "It means the field is still open."

"Not to me!" Lazarus exclaimed. He tried to control his voice. "For me, the field is never open. I can't think of it. I can't allow myself to think of it."

"Are you in love with her?" the father asked again.

"What difference does it make?" asked Lazarus. "What good could come of it even if I were? I have nothing to offer a woman, Daddy . . . an early widowhood. A brief life with an invalid, and then a long period of mourning. I wouldn't wish that on my worst enemy, much less someone I care about." He kept his head down, staring at his feet rather than meeting his father's bright eyes. "Please don't. It's not like you to push me where my mind can't bear to go. I swallow it, that's all; I learned to swallow it long ago. I closed the door on all that. . . . But if you would really like to help my cousin, I have an idea. Will you listen to it, at least?"

The father folded his hands over the coverlet, as he had once folded them at business meetings when he needed to pay close attention. "I am listening," he said cautiously.

"I would like to put a little wind in her sails."

"What do you mean?" asked Mr. Sachs. "Exactly?"

"I'd like to give her more choices than women generally have open to them. More freedom. Libby wants to learn. She wants to see the world. I'd like her to have the money to do all that."

"You're a good boy," said Mr. Sachs. "I'm glad you thought of her. But I thought of it too. I've left her five thousand pounds."

"That's very generous, Daddy. But I'd like to do . . . a bit more. Quite a bit more. I'd like to kick the door open wide."

Something in his son's tone struck the old man, as it had sometimes at a bargaining table when negotiations turned unexpectedly difficult. Mr. Sachs kept a neutral voice now, as he always had then. "Go on," he said, refolding his hands.

"Libby is poor," said Lazarus. "She doesn't realize how poor. Mother made her show some bank papers and things. Her father spent nearly everything and died in debt. I don't want her to have to become a clerk in a store—or something else equally unsuitable. We've seen she wouldn't make much of a nurse."

Both men smiled.

"And I don't want her to have to marry in order to survive. I don't want her to struggle in that way. I'd like to make her rich."

"So you do love her!" exclaimed Mr. Sachs.

Lazarus looked pained. "Daddy, please."

"What do you mean by rich?"

"I'd say someone is rich when they can do as they like. Broadly speaking. When they can live, not just by filling a need but by feeding their imagination. Libby has a great deal of imagination."

"So do you, apparently," said the father. He had begun to feel almost dizzy. He wondered if he might be dreaming the whole conversation. But no, his son was still sitting there, very close, a hungry expression on his face.

"Think of it as an interest I will have when—when—"

"But people are not hobbies," said the father. "Have you thought this out? Aren't you afraid you might be putting Libby in harm's way? If I give her . . ." he hesitated.

"Half. I would like her to have half of my share."

The old man shook his head. He allowed himself to look and feel pained, just a moment. "Half will be more than two hundred thousand pounds. That's as much as some Astors and Rockefellers make."

"Libby is worth any number of Astors and Rockefellers," Lazarus declared.

"It's enough to get the attention of some scoundrel. There are people in this world as determined to be bad as others are to be good. Right now her poverty protects her, in a manner of speaking."

"It also limits her. Her choices are frighteningly narrow."

"But the risks for a young heiress are frighteningly real. And she wasn't raised to be wary of them. I half think she wasn't raised at all. She's like one of those wild children raised by wolves. She could fall prey to any number of ugly schemes."

Lazarus crossed his legs and rested his long hands on top of his knees. "That is a risk I am prepared to take," he said.

Mr. Sachs closed his eyes. "You frighten me when you say that."

"Why?" When Mr. Sachs didn't answer, the young man leaned forward and spoke gently. "Why, Father?"

Mr. Sachs kept his eyes closed. It was clear that this conversation had tired him out very much; it was drawing to an end, as it must. "Because it isn't your risk to take. . . . I wonder what my sister would want me to do, if she were alive."

"You told me your sister cherished her freedom," argued Lazarus.

"Yes, and look where it got her. A bad marriage. Dead at an early age . . ."

"Would she have sacrificed her freedom to choose?" asked Lazarus.

"You are too clever," said Mr. Sachs. "You could always out-argue me. You would have made a fine lawyer. A politician. So many possibilities." He held out one trembling hand, and Lazarus took it and brought it up to his cheek. Both men would have been horrified had anyone witnessed this display of emotion. But they were alone together, as they had very often been. "I could leave you all the money and let you divide it with her."

"Daddy," said Lazarus. "Be sensible. I can't give Libby my own money. Think how it would look."

"It's yours in any event," said Mr. Sachs.

"But she won't know that. She mustn't ever find out."

"She may guess it." He shrugged. "As you wish," said Mr. Sachs. "I'll call my lawyer, Smallman. I should probably call in a psychiatrist instead. This is the second time you've had me revise the will to cheat yourself. Are you very sure about all this?"

"As sure as I've ever been of anything."

The old man smiled at his son's eager expression. "That's something, at least. That degree of certainty."

Lazarus kissed his father's hand. "Thank you," he said simply.

"You know . . . you yourself may not always be around to protect her. From the chances, as you say. And the consequences."

"All the more reason," said Lazarus. "To do our best for her while we can."

Over the next few days, Libby and Clara Merle were thrown much into each other's company. Their affection and friendship increased. Mrs. Sachs was busy consulting with doctors who came in an endless stream to Gardencourt. None of them had anything hopeful to offer. The house was so quiet you could hear the ticking of its clocks, like so many heartbeats. Lazarus stayed away from the two women entirely.

"My poor cousin," said Libby. "He must be beside himself."

"He would avoid me in any case," said Madame Merle. "He doesn't care for my company."

"Then he must not know you. Not well."

Clara's smile quirked up to the right side in the odd, lopsided way it had. In a strange way, her smile aged her, Libby thought. It almost made her look like the victim of a stroke.

"Or perhaps he knows me too well." Madame Merle smoked a pack a day, and she lit another cigarette now and fit it into a long tortoise-shell cigarette holder. "In any event, it's lucky Lazarus is as ill as he is. It gives him something to do, or an excuse to do nothing. . . . It's always been his calling card."

Libby, dismayed, said nothing. Now and then her new friend, who could be so tender and thoughtful, seemed callous. Clara Merle read her expression. "That sounded hard . . . I only meant," said the older woman, "your American men seem to lose themselves when they come abroad—even if, like your cousin, they are brought here at an early age, through no fault of their own. But they end up stuck here, in Europe, with too little to sustain them. No work, no title, no cause, no identity to speak of . . ."

"You sound like my friend Henrietta," said Libby, half smiling. "But I'm sure my cousin would never have chosen his illness as his profession—much less his identity."

"I'm sure not," agreed Madame Merle. "Surely he had ambitions once. God knows I did! I was very ambitious once upon a time. You can't imagine my dreams of grandeur. It's embarrassing to think of it now."

Libby studied her new friend, her gold hair illuminated around her head like a halo in the soft Irish air, under lamplight, her neck firm and white. She suddenly pictured her with a crown on that fine head. *What had she wished to be?* Libby wondered.

"I know a brilliant man in Rome," Clara went on. "A sad case. He has nothing that he should have liked—nothing, nothing. Yet he was capable of anything. He has the most discerning mind I've ever known. His name is Gilbert Osmond. He is a marvel. I wish you could meet him. But he lives in seclusion, and the world knows nothing of him—though he knows all there is to be known about the world."

"Does he live by himself?" asked Libby, interested.

"Well," said Madame Merle, looking down. "He has a young daughter, whom he adores."

"Then he does have at least one thing that he likes," said Libby.

"The daughter, you mean. Yes," said Clara Merle slowly. "But I'm not sure it's what he would have chosen—even the exquisite girl. He could have accomplished so much in his life. He paints a little, creates watercolors and so on. But—I'll give him credit for that—he never does talk about his watercolors. Whereas I am always flaunting my little accomplishments."

"No, you don't," said Libby. "I can barely get you to say two words about yourself. And your accomplishments so far as I can tell are immense."

Madame Merle clapped her hands together. This was a habit with her, to move a conversation along. "Never mind that. I didn't mean for our talk to turn dreary. You must have your own plans. At least I hope you do! It's so important, in this day and age, to have a scheme, or you will find yourself with an apron tied around your waist, a Pontiac in the garage, and two-point-five children fastened around your feet."

"I would love to have children someday."

Madame Merle's sky-blue eyes were bright. "But not yet."

"No, not yet," admitted Libby.

"Good. You must first have your opportunities!"

Libby moved closer to the fire, reaching out to the small white dog. The animal's warm body gave her comfort. Madame Merle made her feel both brave and frightened. She wondered where Lazarus had disappeared to. He showed himself only late at night, after Clara Merle had turned in for the evening. Perhaps he really did dislike her aunt's friend. But why? She spoke hesitantly. "I have had—a few opportunities already," she admitted.

"I take it you mean suitors," said Clara Merle. "Were they clever? Were they rich?"

"I wouldn't care about either," said Libby. "They are both very kind."

"By which I suppose you mean they were nonentities," said Clara, with her crooked smile.

"Not at all," flashed Libby. "One was an English lord." She couldn't help but register a certain pleasure at the surprise on Clara Merle's passive face. "And the other is the best man I know. He's capable of anything. He is the most interesting man too, if I think about it. But I try not to think about it, because I still have so much to learn. So much to see of life itself—not to be attached to any one person. Women rush into love, and then there's no backing out again."

Clara removed a small bit of tobacco from her lips with two firm white fingers. "Just don't wait too long," said Clara. "That was not my problem. I did rush in—and lived to regret it. . . . But one can regret the opposite just as easily. Oh, not the way they say it in the ladies' magazines. 'Beyond the age of twenty-two, a woman's charms significantly diminish,' and so on. Life is not something you can map out. If it were, I'd be a great deal further along. I would have made an excellent general in a war campaign, if planning and strategizing were all there was to it. Or courage, even. I've always had courage. But you can say no once too often, Libby. You can live past your buy-by date, and find yourself sitting damply on some back shelf, wondering where you took the wrong turn. You mustn't wait too long."

"Perhaps you're right," said Libby slowly.

"But you don't think so!" laughed Madame Merle. "Very well, my young friend." She crossed the room and impulsively adjusted and readjusted Libby's hair. "How lovely you are!" There was something genuinely motherly in the gesture, and Libby felt it in the core and marrow of her being. "Only I don't want you to remember my words down the road and say, I wish I had listened to that clever, moldy Madame Merle."

Just then the front door of Gardencourt opened, there was murmuring in the hall, and the latest doctor, the most trusted one, made his exit from the house. He had taken his hat from his head, and he walked slowly, thoughtfully, to his car, and when he pulled the driver's door shut, it made a heavy sound.

"I'd better just step out and see your aunt," said Madame Merle, who went out quietly.

Libby sat alone by the fire, looking out the window, stroking the head of the small white dog. She watched the Irish wind blow in patterns back and forth along the long grass behind Gardencourt. It made the air seem visible, a kind of intricate, ghostly dance. The grass was furred with frost and overgrown. She shivered without knowing why.

At last the door to the parlor opened and Lazarus entered without a trace of his usual smile. He seemed to have aged; his lank white hair falling over his forehead now looked like that of an old man. His hands were sunk in his pockets. "It's all over," he said simply.

Libby went and put her arms around him. "My poor darling," she said.

Chapter Ten

Madame Merle stopped in front of the Paris apartment where she had first met Libby Archer. It was a registered and historic building, with a small blue circular sign attesting to that fact, the portico carved of marble so fluidly it might have been made out of something softer, like soap, with veins of rosy-pink running through it. It was the sort of palatial apartment that many visitors—Clara Merle included—would have given their eyeteeth to own. Mrs. Sachs used it as a pied-à-terre—a stepping stone between Italy, where she spent most of her time, and Ireland, where she had spent as little time as possible over the past twenty years.

As Clara finished paying the taxi fare, she noticed a new sign declaring the property up for sale, in French and in English. "They waste no time," she said to herself before she rang the bell. She was wearing her black Chanel suit with a crisp white shirt. Even here in Paris, her appearance was striking and drew admiring glances from the passersby.

Mrs. Sachs opened the door and they kissed each other on both cheeks, in cosmopolitan style. Mrs. Sachs of course was also wearing black, but her appearance was almost untidy, for once.

"I know," she said without preamble. "You're surprised I'm selling the place so soon. But I am trying to lighten the load."

"Nothing you do will ever surprise me," said Clara Merle. "But how are you getting on?"

"I am surviving," said Mrs. Sachs. "My husband was a good man. I think he came to feel I was a good wife . . . at least, he told me so at the end. I hope I helped him to be a better man as well."

"You gave him many opportunities to sacrifice himself," said Madame Merle, with her strange, crooked smile.

"We lived so much apart. Daniel understood the necessity of that. We were connected, even if we didn't live as other couples do. But he knew that, even in my foreign life, my life abroad, I never showed the slightest preference for anyone else."

"No," said Madame Merle in an undertone, moving around the room, taking in the breathtaking views for the last time. "Only for yourself."

"What was that?" asked Mrs. Sachs. "I can say this much, at least. I never once sacrificed my husband for anyone else."

"Oh certainly not," said Madame Merle, as quietly as before, speaking into the glass of the window, so that only her breath recorded that she had spoken aloud. "You've never done anything for anyone else." Then, in an audible voice, "Will it sell quickly, do you think?"

"Heavens yes. We've already had two offers above the asking price. Nineteen fifty-four was a good year for real estate, and 1955 promises to be better. My husband chose this property himself. He had remarkably good luck in business."

"And none in his private life," Madame Merle murmured.

"Am I going deaf, or are you mumbling?" snapped Mrs. Sachs. "I think my ears have closed from the plane. I bring chewing gum, but it does no good." She lifted a small Lalique vase and put it down again. "I shall ship a few things—but only a few. He left me this apartment, but of course I have a much better one in Rome. Lazarus has Gardencourt; he would never leave Ireland for long. My husband was very generous to a few charities, but that's as one would expect. However there was one oddity," she added after a pause. "He left our niece, Libby, a fortune."

"A fortune!" Clara Merle swung around, her hands clasped.

"Yes, Libby comes into something like two hundred thousand pounds."

Madame Merle's pale-blue eyes dilated. Her hands, still clasped, rose to her breast. "Ah, the clever creature!"

"There was no cleverness involved," said Mrs. Sachs shortly. "The girl is stunned."

Clara Merle's color rose; at the same time she dropped her gaze. "It certainly is clever to achieve such results—with no effort at all."

Mrs. Sachs frowned. "There was no effort involved, I assure you."

Madame Merle smiled, to cover a number of combating instincts—cynicism, envy, disappointment. But she had expected nothing from old Mr. Sachs, surely. "There was nothing between us like that," she would have told her friends, snapping her fingers. "Now his son might have been a different story." Instead, to Mrs. Sachs she simply said, "Libby would not have stepped into a fortune had she not been the most lovable, charming girl in the world. That's a form of cleverness, surely."

"She was my husband's niece, and an orphan," she said. "They were fond of each other; one could see that. She was the child of his only sister. Whatever she achieved, she did unconsciously. She's with me now—Lazarus has gone down to the Riviera for his health. And as for cleverness, at the moment she's just stupefied."

"Is she?"

"She doesn't know what to think. It's as if someone fired a cannon behind her, and she's checking to see if she's still in one piece. When the solicitor made his little speech to her, Libby burst into tears. The principal will remain in an Irish bank, and she's to draw interest monthly."

"How delicious!" Madame Merle touched her lips. "After she's drawn the money a few times, she'll get used to it. The shock will wear off and something else will settle in its place." A thought suddenly occurred to her. "How is Lazarus taking it?"

"He's devastated, of course. He adored his father; they were two peas in a pod." Madame Merle made a gesture of impatience, which Mrs. Sachs registered. "Oh, do you mean about the money? Yes, some of his inheritance went to Libby. I don't think he minds it. He's never minded anything his father did."

"Perhaps he even suggested it," said Clara Merle, her eyes large and bright.

"It's more likely he'd have suggested the money go to *me*," said Mrs. Sachs. "In any event, it's not the kind of thing that we would discuss. Lazarus is not a young man who's always thinking about number one."

"That might depend on who he thinks of as number one," remarked Clara. "Am I to see your happy niece while I'm in Paris?"

"Don't expect to find her happy," said Mrs. Sachs. "Good God—it would be unseemly. And Libby is never that. But she is genuinely somber these days—as if she's carrying the weight of the world on her shoulders."

"I suppose so," mused Clara. "I would like very much to see her. May I?"

"Of course," Mrs. Sachs answered irritably. "We will be at the usual Paris salons, once a few months have passed."

"Yes of course," said Clara. "Nothing must get in the way of that!"

❧

Those few months later, Libby was standing at the foot of a gilded Paris staircase, looking like a very different young woman than the one who had been packing boxes in her late father's house in Rochester, New York. Her dress was Parisian. It tied at the waist with a simple white satin ribbon. Her hairstyle too was à la mode in Paris—shorter and sleeker, all the rage in 1955. She had traded her Moondrops lipstick for a paler shade of mauvey pink. Yet she looked somber indeed, like someone wearing a costume that was a few pounds too heavy, too stiff. She was smiling with helpless politeness at the small group of women—fellow expatriates, all of them at least ten or fifteen years her senior—who encircled her.

"I can get you the name of my manicurist," said the plumpest of the circle. "She does everything comme il faut. There is even a name for these white tips. They call it a French manicure."

"I would like her number as well," put in the woman standing next to her.

"I carry her card for this purpose," said the plump woman, smiling benignly. "It isn't easy to get an appointment. One must plan well ahead."

"We could use a fourth for bridge on Wednesdays," said the eldest of the group. She wore her white hair in an avant-garde swoop. It was said that she collected monographs and knew something about modern art.

"That's very kind," answered Libby, "but I don't play bridge."

"If you have a quick mind, you will pick it up quickly," said the bridge player. "And if you don't"—she glanced severely at one or two in the circle—"you'll never learn at all. But I think you will be a quick study," she added more kindly.

"I don't know how long we will be in Paris," said Libby. "I would hate to disappoint you."

"Oh, none of us ever knows how long we will be here in Paris!" laughed another woman. "I thought I would be here for a month or two. And that was in 1943!"

The other women laughed with her. And then the plump woman said, more seriously, "It is not so easy to find a group like ours. Times have changed. Manners, expectations. Just look at all the trouble with the Algerians! Unthinkable a few years ago. We must replace Mendès France with a more sensible point of view."

At that moment Henrietta swooped in. If Libby was notable for how much she had changed, Henry was as distinguished for how absolutely she had stayed the same. She was now a European correspondent for the papers at home, but that was a change in title and location only. Paris had not touched her. "Are you ready to go?" she asked Libby.

"Almost," Libby said. "My aunt doesn't like to wait up much past nine."

"Thirty minutes," Henry said, tapping her watch, and off she went. Libby watched her stride off, rather enviously.

"We must protect our interests in Indochine," said the plump woman. "Despite what others say."

"I never discuss politics," said the white-haired woman. "I hear they have a folksinger tonight. I hope he won't sing political songs."

"A folksinger!" exclaimed a thin woman with thin, sharp lips. "What on earth is that?"

"Very current," said the plump woman. "And besides," she added, shrugging, "anything for a change."

❧

"I know that young man," said Libby to Henry, as the salon gathered around the evening's musician. He was singing "Bound for Glory" in a thin, reedy but pleasant voice. No one had quite stopped their talking to listen to him, but they had lowered their voices.

"We all know that young man," Henry whispered back. "At least back home we do."

"No, I mean I know him personally—I feel as if I must," said Libby.

He was barely out of his teens, and he wore his hair long, under a black cap with a brim. Had he been wearing a black motorcycle jacket, the effect of the long hair might have been menacing, but he was sensitive to his audience, and when he felt their attention wander, or their hackles rise, he settled down into something more cheerful. In fact, he would have suited a school uniform far better than the leather jacket—and then Libby had it.

"It's little Ned Rosier!" she declared. "Our fathers were friends," said Libby. "One summer at Canandaigua they rescued me when my father disappeared for a week. Ned was a little angel then, with china-blue eyes. Oh, he's combed back all his golden curls!" She smiled and waved, and the young man burst into a smile. He waggled the guitar by way of greeting and swung into "Goodnight, Irene."

As soon as he had finished the song, he made his way through the lukewarm crowd, nodding and smiling to each, came straight to Libby, and seized her hands in a way that turned Henrietta's heart toward him.

"I thought it was you!" he cried. "You have gotten very beautiful. But *mon Dieu*," he added in perfect French. "*Je suis désolé. Ton papa . . . très triste.* My father told me of your loss."

"I thought you were American," said Henry.

"I spent half my life here and half in America," Ned answered gravely.

Henry narrowed her bright, buttonlike eyes on Ned. "But you were singing American folk songs. So you must have some sense of attachment to your own land."

Ned smiled his most winning smile. "I am loyal to music itself," he said. "Now tell me, is it true, Libby? Papa had heard you were engaged to marry Caspar Lockwood."

"Aha!" said Henrietta. "I like your music better already."

"Thank you," said Ned.

"It is not true," said Libby.

Ned's face fell slightly. "*Tant pis.* The man is a genius. He was changing the face of music, he had made great strides, and the man who changes the music can change the whole culture. That at least is my opinion," he added. "Jazz, the blues, country music, the folk songs, the great singers like Johnny Ray. Do you know what he said?" Without waiting for their answer, he went on. "He said, 'I make them feel. I exhaust them; I destroy them.' Isn't that wonderful?"

"Charming," said Henrietta.

"But your Mr. Lockwood has turned to computers now. There's no future in that. He was on the right track with music. Do you think he'll go back to working on improving the LP?"

"He's not my Mr. Lockwood," said Libby.

"More's the pity," answered Ned.

"On that we agree," said Henry. "She might have made something great of him. The two of them together would be a force."

"Indeed!" said the young man agreeably.

"*Pardon*," said a clear, mellow voice behind them. It was Madame Merle. Her hair was swept back in a smooth blonde chignon; small diamond earrings glittered at her ears. The effect was dazzling, and silenced even Ned. Libby made the introductions, and Ned bent his head over Madame Merle's firm white hand and kissed it.

Clara and Henrietta regarded each other coolly. "How are you?" asked Clara indifferently.

"I'm here. Right here," answered Henry.

"Yes, of course you are. And my dear friend," said Clara, embracing Libby. "We have not really spoken since your great loss—"

"I'm glad to see you."

"It's been too long. I've been away." Clara held the younger woman by the shoulders, peered into her eyes, and then kissed her rapidly, once on each cheek. Ned had begun talking again to Henry about music, and Clara murmured to Libby, "But we must spend some time alone together. How about tomorrow at the Café d'Étoile? It's near your aunt's, a quiet place; shall we say eleven o'clock?" Libby nodded. "Good—I must be off. Salons don't really suit me. You added something new," she said to Ned. "I must thank you for that."

"Oh—well—you're very welcome," he said, flustered. "I'm always looking for new places to play," he added hopefully.

"I'm sure you will find them," she answered, and turned away without saying goodbye to Henrietta.

Henry watched her go. "I don't care for that woman," she said.

"Ned, we must have a meal together in Paris," Libby said hurriedly. She had a rather guilty feeling now that she had an appointment to dine alone with Clara Merle, a guilt she hid by digging into her purse for a card, on which she scribbled busily with a pen. "You'll be around for a little while longer, won't you?"

"Broke, young, footloose, and fancy-free," said Ned, hoisting his guitar. "It's a good time to be alive, ladies!" He kissed his hand to them and made his way into the crowd, accepting compliments as he went and snaring canapés.

"He was always a sweet boy," said Libby, somewhat defensively.

"Oh, I don't mind him," said Henry. "He has a cause, at least. But we'd better get you home, before it's too late."

"Too late for what?" asked Libby.

"I'm not sure," admitted Henry. "Let's start by getting you home, and then I'll let you know."

"I'm ready," said Libby. "We have time to walk back to my aunt's."

"That's not what I meant, and you know it," said Henry.

Madame Merle was waiting with an amused smile the next morning when Libby came cautiously through the doors of the café wearing tortoise-shell sunglasses.

"Are you in disguise?" she asked, kissing her friend and relieving her of her jacket. "Am I so risqué?"

"Oh! No, of course not," answered Libby, blushing and laughing.

"But you can't stay long. You're on a very tight leash. I understand," said Madame Merle.

"My aunt is still in mourning," answered Libby.

"Yet she's been taking you to all the Paris stores," Clara Merle observed, nodding at Libby's pale-pink outfit. It featured a soft black bow at the neck and a slim, woven pink-and-black skirt. "Le Bazar de l'Hôtel de Ville. Very chic."

"You don't like it much," said Libby, glancing down. "Neither do I."

"I like the Bazar's escalator." Madame Merle quirked her lips. "But surely you are now free . . . to dress as you please? To suit your own taste?"

"All the more reason to please my aunt," said Libby. "Since it matters so little to me, and so much to her."

"You are too kind," murmured Clara, patting her friend's hand. "Will you have an éclair? They're very good here. And you've lost weight. You need to plump up."

"I'm not fond of sweets," said Libby.

"Good. Then come to Italy."

Libby stared. "I beg your pardon?"

"You've had your fill of Paris now . . . and from the look of it, you're ready for the next thing. You've blossomed beautifully but you've been through a great deal—a great change. I think Rome would suit you perfectly."

"Why?" asked Libby, pretending to study the menu. Compliments always made her blush.

"There's a reason they call Rome the Eternal City," answered Clara. "Rome possesses mystery and depth. You can never fathom it entirely; you can never use it up. It is civilized. Genuinely civilized. There are a few people I would very much like you to meet. And I think your poor aunt will be much happier once she's back among her own things and people."

"Do you really think so?" asked Libby. "That alone would be reason to go to Italy."

A waiter came to the table, and Clara ordered rapidly in French. The waiter bowed and retreated.

"I have taken the liberty," said Clara, "of ordering you a real French breakfast."

"But you must let me treat you."

Clara waved her hand airily. She wore, as always, a number of sparkling rings on her fingers. "Only come to Rome as soon as you can. You must be tired of hotels. And call me the moment you get there." She pressed a card into Libby's hand. "The number on the back is private. Even your aunt doesn't have that phone number." She slid back her chair and put on a white leather jacket.

"Surely you'll stay and have breakfast?" Libby protested.

"No, *bien sûr*, I must watch my figure," said Clara Merle. "I am getting to the age where one can't be too careful. And I don't wish to interfere in your affairs at such a busy, delicate time. Your aunt wouldn't like it. Nor your watchful American friend, the journalist."

"Henry? She's heading back to the British Isles," said Libby.

"That will suit her best," said Clara, with her funny sideways smile. "But for you, something deeper."

"Rome," breathed Libby.

"Rome," Madame Merle agreed. "There are so few things in life that do not disappoint. Rome never disappoints."

❧

"I hate to leave you here alone," said Henrietta. She was immaculately dressed in her traveling clothes, and the eternal Mr. Pye was waiting patiently outside. He was a shy man and like many shy men, seemed to take great comfort in Henrietta's boldness. "But you know I have to go where I can write my articles. Americans don't want to read about Italy. They still haven't forgiven Mussolini. And France . . ." She pursed her lips ruefully. "Well, France isn't viewed in a much rosier light, to tell the truth. Besides, I've already done Versailles. They can't seem to get enough of the British, however, and Mr. Pye has gotten me an interview with Lady Pensil at her English country house. I'll have enough material for four or five articles, at least. But the idea of you alone in Italy, and in Rome no less. . . . And I suppose you'll have a great deal to do with that Madame Merle."

"I will be staying at my aunt's," said Libby, smiling.

"That's another thing I don't understand. You're free as a bird now—you can go where you please."

"My aunt has made that clear. But I know she appreciates my company, especially after all she's been through. It would be ungrateful of me to desert her. Henry, come and sit down a moment. Try not to fix me, just for a little bit. I want to ask you something."

Henry sat immediately beside her friend on a small blue French sofa, with its curved wooden legs. "What do you want to ask?" Her eyes were clear and large. Libby knew how much she would miss that clear gaze.

"I . . ." But instead of asking the intended question, Libby said, "I'm afraid."

Henry put one hand protectively over her friend's. "Tell me. What are you afraid of?"

Libby tried to laugh. "I think I'm afraid of life itself."

"I've never known you to be fearful," said Henry, drawing back a little, as if to see her friend more clearly. "Though you've often had good reason to be afraid."

"True," admitted Libby. "It's a new sensation. But I've never had my own money before. I've never had any stewardship over anything. I wish cousin Lazarus were here. He's still on the Riviera; it's almost as if he's staying away on purpose. I can't tell if he's upset about his father's will . . ."

"I cannot imagine that," said Henry.

"Neither can I. Which raises the question: Why is he avoiding me? It seems deliberate."

"Surely he's still in mourning for his father," said Henry gently. "You can't blame him for that. He's lost his best friend, his anchor."

"Yes. I know. It's egotistical to think I have anything to do with it. But Henrietta . . . do you think it's good for me to have so much?"

"I don't believe money is good or bad," said Henry, choosing her words carefully. She was always at her most tender on the point of departure. If Mr. Pye had known this, he might have taken his leave of her more often. "It's what you choose to do with your fortune that will make the difference."

"What if I choose badly?"

"My dear friend!" Henry said cheerfully. "It's not in you to be bad!"

"What if I waste my opportunity?" asked Libby. "What if I am never of any use to anyone?"

"That's not in your nature, either, and money shouldn't change your basic composition. It won't if you don't let it. Maybe you don't need to think everything out so much in advance. The right path will be put in front of you. Stretch your wings and fly, this once. You don't have to search hard to find some good to do. Just do . . . whatever comes next."

"You're right," said Libby, brightening. "Money is not an illness. I act as if I'm lying sick in a hospital, and I'm expecting someone to tell me how to get well."

"We have to cure ourselves. Even when we really do get ill." Henry looked at her friend with wide eyes.

"You shouldn't keep Mr. Pye waiting," said Libby. "I've held you here long enough."

"He likes to wait," said Henry. "At least, he says he does, and I don't think Mr. Pye says much that he doesn't mean. It's one of my favorite things about the British. You may say what you like about the Irish, but I don't think they're quite as straightforward." She rose to her feet and smoothed out her dress, tugging at the hem. Her face was troubled. "Libby, I know you are smart . . . but I want you to be wise as well."

"I'll try to be," said Libby. She rose as well, and Henry enveloped her in a hug.

"I hate to let you so far out of my sight!" Henry exclaimed.

"You sound like Mr. Lockwood," Libby said, smiling.

Henry held her friend by the shoulders, almost as if she would shake her. Her tangled hair fell all around her face. "And what about Mr. Lockwood?" she asked. "Does he have no chance at all now?"

"I have to admit," said Libby, "I sometimes think—when I have seen all that I can see, when I have tired myself out . . . there may come a time when the very qualities I am running from in him will seem the best thing in the world: like a clear, quiet harbor enclosed by a granite breakwater. But please don't tell him I said that! Don't tell him anything just yet."

"Well, I'm glad to hear it," said Henry, and she kissed her friend as tenderly as she had ever done in her life.

When Henry had reached the door Libby said, "You'll write to me, won't you?"

"Of course I will," said Henry.

"And Mr. Pye . . ." There was a long moment's hesitation between the two friends. Henry's face, her long sharp nose, was already pointing toward the door. But she turned to look at Libby.

"Is he a good friend to you?" Libby finished lamely.

"A very good friend!" declared Henry, and sailed out the door. Libby watched the swing of Henry's coat billow and settle around her long legs. She listened even for the click of her boot heels down the hall, and hated to admit even to herself how sorry she was to see the brave figure go.

Chapter Eleven

On one of the Seven Hills of Rome, atop the ancient, tree-shaded hill once known as the Palatine, sat a peculiar house. It was peculiar partly for its beauty, made of a golden-colored stone, unusual in that part of Italy, which seemed to glow at sunrise and sunset. Its windows were well proportioned but narrow, massively barred, and placed higher than usual, as if defying passersby to get a glimpse within. What's more, the house was situated so as to seem to sit with its back turned to the street. A casual visitor would not have easily known which was the front door and which the back. However, casual visitors seldom came by to wonder about it.

Within the house, a series of French doors led out to a lush but tangled garden, overgrown with olive trees, thick dark vines, and sweet-smelling roses. It was just that moment in a Roman spring when all the roses seemed to burst into bloom at once. The effect, both inside and out, was charming—one might even say dazzling.

Without appearing to care for organization or luxury, the house made an unforgettable impression, for every item in it had been chosen with care and the most exquisite, if eccentric, taste. Antiquities stood side by side with pieces carved a mere two hundred years earlier, and

Murano, Favrile, and Émile Gallé glass sparkled side by side with mint-green Roman artifacts. Each corner seemed as graceful, as naturally beautiful, as the profusion of flowers outside. Nothing here spoke of the modern world. It is doubtful that any piece dated after the 1920s, and the vulgar 1950s had been banished altogether, with its steely lines, molded plastic, and cheap conveniences. There was no sound or odor of passing motorcars, which were well screened by the house's oblique position and its olive trees. Only an occasional burst of birdsong interrupted the deep quiet within.

The quiet was so complete, in fact, that it had become uncomfortable for the two plump nuns who sat perched at the edge of their chairs as if they had been tacked on there but might at any moment be pried loose and tossed away. Their young charge sat more comfortably on a small sofa, devised as if just for her size, with her feet tucked underneath her. She was smiling, but she too was absolutely silent and motionless.

"This is the most beautiful room I have ever seen!" whispered the younger of the nuns, but her whisper rang out like a shout.

"Shh!" said the older nun, not unkindly but firmly, with a look toward the door.

The master of the house entered just then, his hands behind his back. Gilbert Osmond was a striking man of medium height and medium years, with hazel eyes tilted at the corners. He wore a sharply trimmed Van Dyke beard, and his close-cropped hair was grizzled, giving him a look of distinction and emphasizing the shape of his large, well-formed skull. His profile was as fine as any stamped on a gold coin. He was dressed carelessly, but every item that he wore was immaculate and had once been a thing of beauty—from the fine cotton shirt, now worn to a silken sheen, down to his dark-blue socks encased in worn leather loafers.

"I wonder if I can offer you some refreshment," he said, and his speaking voice was deeper than one might have expected. "I never know what to serve . . . ," he added helplessly.

"No, nothing," said the older nun firmly, in the same instant that the younger said, "Only a glass of water." The younger blushed.

"Of course you may have some water," said the elder.

"We have excellent water here," said the man. "But we also have cakes."

"Just the water," said the older nun. "Thank you."

The father caught his young daughter's gaze. She was looking at a watercolor painting on its easel. "What do you think of it, *cara*?" he asked.

"I like it very much," she declared. "Did you make it, Papa?"

He glanced at it carelessly. "I did. Do you think I'm clever?"

"The cleverest man in the world. I too have learned how to make pictures."

"I wish you had brought a few samples to show me."

"I brought lots of them. They're all in my suitcase, well wrapped up." She moved her hands to demonstrate how carefully they had been wrapped. All three adults looked at her fondly. She seemed much younger than her age, and her voice was a clear, high child's voice. Her hair fell in bright-golden curls over her shoulders. The effect, however, was not like Shirley Temple's popular banana curls, but something much more subtle and artfully old-fashioned.

The man poured the water into cut crystal glasses and handed them to the sisters, first the elder, then the younger. He lifted a third glass to offer one to his daughter but she shook her head. "No thank you, Papa. I had a *limonade* on the train." Another silence fell.

"She draws very—carefully," said the elder nun. "*Minutieusement*," she added in French.

"Are you her drawing teacher?" asked the man.

"Happily, *non*," said the sister, blushing a little. "That is not my gift."

"We have a German drawing master," said the younger nun. "He has been with us for many years. He is excellent with the children."

"But you yourselves are French," said the man.

"Oh yes, we are like a United Nations at the school," said the younger nun eagerly.

"But no Russians, I hope," he said. "One must draw the line somewhere."

"No Russians." The older nun looked blinkingly at her host. "Though we do have sisters from all over the world: English, German, Belgian, Irish."

"And has the Irishwoman been teaching my daughter how to clean?" he asked with a smile. When neither woman seemed to understand the joke, he added, "You're very complete, it seems."

"Yes, we choose everything of the best for the young ones," said the older nun.

"Even gymnastics," added the younger, plumper one. "But not dangerous."

"I should hope not. Is gymnastics *your* specialty?" he asked, and now both women did laugh.

The girl, as if released by the sound, got up and wandered over to the locked door leading to the garden.

"She's grown this year," said the man.

"Yes," said the older nun. "But she will remain petite." She gestured with her hands.

"She has been such a pleasure to teach," said the younger. "So sweet."

"I am not truly sorry she is small," said the man. "I like women to be like books—good, but not too long. Though there is no reason that she should be slight. Her mother was not."

Both sisters bowed their heads. Then the older nun said, "Well, she has good health, that's the important thing, thank God."

"Yes, she seems sound enough." He walked up to his daughter, who was still gazing out into the garden. "What's caught your attention out there?"

"I see a lot of flowers," she said in her small, sweet voice. She seemed a little frightened, as if about to be tested.

"The best of them have come and gone," he said. "Our season is short. But go ahead and gather as many as you can for *ces dames*." And he unlocked the door.

The girl looked up at him, as if to a great height, and beamed with pleasure. "May I, really?"

"If I say so," answered the father.

She glanced at the elder nun. "May I indeed, *ma mère*?"

"Always obey *monsieur*, your father, my child," said the nun, reddening. Released, the girl descended into the garden and vanished out of sight.

"Well, you don't spoil them!" the man said.

"They must ask permission for everything," she explained. "That is our system."

"It's an excellent system. It is why I chose you over all others for my daughter. I have every faith you will continue to do well by her."

"One must always have faith," said the younger. She had finished her water and looked around helplessly now for a place to put the crystal glass. She seemed reluctant to hold the precious object any longer than required. Yet when he took it from her, she seemed equally reluctant to let it go.

"That is what we wish to talk to you about," said the elder nun.

"I hope there are no problems? Viola has not been causing any trouble?"

Both sisters seemed shocked into speechlessness. Then the elder spoke. "Viola is perfect. She has no faults."

"Well, she had none when I gave her to you. I'm glad you are bringing her back untouched. I think I can keep her for the summer without danger. She seems *gentille*. And she's a pretty little thing."

"Not so little anymore," said the elder nun. "A convent is not *comme le monde, monsieur*. We have had her since she was so small. We've done the best we could."

"Of all the ones we will lose this year, we will miss Viola the most," said the younger one tearfully. "We love her like our own."

"Why must you lose her?" said the father.

"She is nearly fifteen years old, *monsieur*. It is time for her to enter the world now. She is one of the oldest in the convent."

"And the sweetest," added the younger one.

"The younger girls look up to her. We will never forget her. We will speak of her often." The older nun polished her spectacles, while the other one frankly blew her nose and wiped her eyes.

"I see," said the man. He crossed over to a small desk and busied himself with some papers there. "I suppose we could try her at home this summer, on a trial basis . . ."

"A trial?" fumbled the younger sister, through her handkerchief.

"One must be sure of doing the right thing," said the father. "I assume you would not turn her away, if she needed to return? Nor turn down the fees?"

"We want only what is best for the child," said the older nun, fitting her spectacles back on, and looking rather more closely than before at the father. "But I am convinced you will find she belongs here in the real world, with you."

"This," he looked around him, "is not the real world. I make sure of that. But I will take it under consideration, certainly. She may be as easy as she is good."

The younger sister clasped her hands and leaned forward. "You can't imagine how good, *monsieur*. You simply can't imagine! I wish we could keep Viola forever."

"If it were entirely up to me, you could," said the father.

"Good as she is," said the elder nun, "she was made for the world. And the world will gain by having such a perfect young lady in it."

"The world has a habit of ruining perfection," remarked the man.

"But there are good people everywhere," put in the younger.

The man rose abruptly. "Well, when you depart, there will be two less of them here," he said.

The two nuns jumped to their feet with embarrassment. "We have kept you too long," said the bespectacled nun, looking reproachfully at the empty water glasses, as if they were to blame for their own luxury.

"Not at all, not at all," the man said. But he moved swiftly to the door leading out to the garden and clapped his hands.

"Bring the flowers," he called. "The sisters must be going now." He half turned. "Will you take the train back tonight?" he asked indifferently.

"Yes, we have so much to do."

The girl appeared as if she had flown to the door. In one hand she carried a large bouquet of pink roses, in the other white. She had artfully arranged other flowers as well—blue lupine and pale-gold lilies. She went to the older nun first. "Will you choose?" she pleaded. "They are exactly the same, except the color of the roses."

The elder nun smiled at the younger. "You choose, sister. You care more than I do for color and beauty."

"Oh no, I couldn't," answered the other, blushing.

"I will choose then," said the father smoothly, handing the pink flowers to the elder and the white to the younger. Both sisters murmured their thanks, and the younger nun buried her nose in the roses.

"I will be breathing these all the way home," she told the girl.

"I wish I could give you something that would last!" cried Viola.

"We mustn't keep the good sisters waiting," said the father impatiently. He walked to open the door while the sisters embraced the girl and said their goodbyes, with tears on both sides. The man looked over their heads.

The girl stood quivering as she watched them go, rising up on her tiptoes to see them pass out of sight, down the front path, and away. "I will miss you!" she called. Her father stood with his shoulder to her, also watching them go.

"You must learn to be less emotional," he said, when he was sure they were alone again.

"Yes, Papa," she said.

"It isn't good for you."

"I'm sure you are right," she said. She stood in the center of the room, as if unsure where to go next. He busied himself with something by the entrance, some figurines whose placement no longer pleased him.

The girl caught her breath with a little gasp. "There's someone out in our garden!" she said.

"Perhaps a workman," he said. "The garden doesn't keep itself, you know."

"I think it's a lady," observed Viola. "She looks like a moving statue. She is trying to hold still."

"A moving—" He went impatiently to the open door and saw something that made him jerk his head back for an instant. Then he went out into the garden.

A woman glided forward silently. When she had drawn quite close she asked, "Is anyone here?"

"Someone you are allowed to see."

She entered the house noiselessly.

Viola let out a soft cry, not exactly of welcome. "Oh, it's Madame Merle!"

The woman held out her two hands, and the girl came forward timidly. At the very last instant she put up her face to be kissed.

"I came to welcome you home," said Madame Merle.

"That was kind of you," said Viola. "Though you visited me just last month."

The man turned his head quickly to the side. "Did she?"

"Yes, I had to be in France on other business," said Madame Merle smoothly. "I brought you a little muff, do you remember? But I expect it's too warm to need it now."

"I remember you said I'd be leaving the convent soon," said Viola.

"Is that right?" the child's father asked.

"I don't remember. I suppose I knew she'd be coming home for summer vacation. All children like vacations, don't they?"

"Viola, go into the garden and pick some flowers for Madame Merle," he said.

"If it won't tire you, after your journey," added Madame Merle.

"Oh no, I love the garden. I am happy to go."

"I'm glad the nuns have taught you to be obedient," said Madame Merle. "That's what all good little girls must learn."

"Yes, and bigger girls as well," said the father. "It is essential—the most essential thing."

"I have high grades in obedience always," said Viola. "But I'm afraid the nicest flowers are already gone."

"The nuns beat you to it," Osmond told Madame Merle. The two adults stood close together, without touching. They spoke in low voices, not with any great intimacy, or even out of necessity, for they were saying nothing that Viola couldn't hear, but rather as if out of long habit.

"Shall I go out now?" asked Viola.

"In a moment." Madame Merle approached. She took Viola's hand and looked at the small, delicate fingers lying in her own hand, as if reading the girl's palm. "I hope the nuns always made you wear gloves," she said. "Though I hated them when I was a child."

"I like them," said Viola.

"Good! Then I'll buy you a dozen pair!"

"In all pretty colors?"

Madame Merle laughed. "Are you fond of pretty, colorful things?"

"Yes—but just a little," said Viola, rather primly.

"Then they will be just a little pretty," said Madame Merle, dropping her hand. The girl skipped quickly away.

"Run out to the garden now," said her father.

The two adults stood facing into the garden, watching her go. Then Madame Merle turned to Osmond. "Do you think she will miss Mother Catherine?" she asked.

"Who?"

"The elder nun. The one with the glasses."

"Oh," he said. "I have no idea. I suppose so."

"You must discourage that," she said.

"Must I?"

"Perhaps one day she'll have another mother."

"I don't see why. She has about twenty of them at the convent."

Clara Merle shrugged with impatience. She was wearing a full, belted silk dress the color of a soft summer sky. The blue brought out the blue in her eyes, and the paleness of her frosted hair, nearly white-blonde, as was the fashion. "I would have hoped you'd driven to France and gotten Viola yourself."

Osmond picked up the two empty crystal glasses and brought them over to a small sink—an artist's sink, made for washing out brushes—and began to wash them carefully.

"I am an indifferent driver," he said.

"That's what I want to talk to you about."

He raised his eyebrows. "My driving?"

"Your indifference."

He dried his hands carefully on a soft linen towel, then set the crystal goblets upside-down to air dry. "Isn't it a little late," he asked, "to complain about my indifference?"

Madame Merle kept her eyes on the girl out in the garden. Viola moved uncertainly from bush to bush. "I am not speaking on my own behalf, but on yours."

"So you've always said," he answered.

She turned on him with an uncharacteristic flame in her pale-blue eyes. "And you doubt me still?" Her hands were clenched. With an effort, she loosened them, and when she spoke again, her voice had regained its usual smoothness. "I want you to make an effort."

Osmond threw himself into a chair, stretched his long legs, and crossed them at the ankles. "You have to remember how lazy I am."

"I beg you to forget it."

Osmond raised his eyebrows. "You beg me? That's new."

"I wish to God that it were," she said with her lopsided smile.

They were interrupted by the reentry of Viola, who approached hesitantly, holding a handful of lilies and a few blood-red roses. "I didn't know what you would like," said the girl, hanging back.

"I'll like whatever you give me, because it comes from you," said Madame Merle, beckoning her to come closer. Once again, Viola approached and lifted her forehead to be kissed, with a dutiful expression. Madame Merle stooped to bestow the kiss, but then turned aside at the last moment.

"You don't much like to be kissed, do you?" she asked.

"I don't mind," the girl said bravely.

"But look, she's bleeding!" Madame Merle said, with real concern.

"It was only a little hidden thorn," said Viola.

"Don't you have a Band-Aid?" Madame Merle swung on Osmond, who had not risen from his chair.

"Of course I do. Upstairs. *Cara*, go on up, and wash off your hand. The box of Band-Aids is under the sink."

"I can go with her," said Madame Merle.

"No," said Osmond. "I haven't raised her to be coddled, and neither have the good sisters. You're able to take care of this yourself, aren't you?" he asked his daughter.

"Bien sûr," said the girl. "Of course I am."

"Good," he said. "Let me look." Viola went obediently to her father and held out her hand. He nodded. "Only a small flesh wound. I think you'll live. Run along now. Don't get blood on the carpet," he added half jovially.

Viola turned to Madame Merle. “I hope you like the flowers,” she said in her high, clipped voice. Then she turned and ran lightly up the stairs, cupping the wounded hand in the other.

“I do, very much!” Clara Merle called after her.

A not altogether affable silence reigned downstairs. Madame Merle found a vase, and arranged the red roses with a judicious eye, adding water from the small tap. The bouquet looked sparse and stiff, no matter how she moved the stems around.

“Dogs and children never take to me,” she said.

“Ah, well. Luckily, I don’t have a dog,” said Osmond, watching her. “Besides, I don’t see such virtue in being liked.”

“Yet I know a young woman who’s recently come into a large fortune, simply from being likable.”

“Oh, well . . . young women do that sort of thing all the time.”

“Don’t be odious,” she said. “That’s what I want to talk to you about.”

“About young women?”

“This particular one. She’s here in Rome, and I would like you to . . . make an effort.”

“What good will it do me?” he asked bluntly.

“It might entertain you,” she said.

“I don’t lack entertainment,” he said. “I don’t relish other people’s society. I’d just as soon be alone.”

“It might do you a great deal of good. You and Viola both.”

He winced. “I could tell this was going to be tiresome. Out with it. Who is this young woman, and why should I care?”

“She’s a niece of Mrs. Sachs. You remember Mrs. Sachs, don’t you?”

“The Jew? I presume the niece is also Jewish?”

“Don’t pretend to be worse than you are,” she said coldly. “You’re bad enough without embellishments.”

“A niece sounds like someone with hair ribbons. Someone who minces when she walks.”

"Libby doesn't mince."

"So she has a name," said Osmond, crossing his arms across his chest.

"Of course she has a name!"

He pretended to consider, then shook his head. "Libby. No. I don't like it."

"Why on earth not?"

"It sounds vulgar."

"She is not the least bit vulgar, I promise you. She is twenty-two or twenty-three, well bred, and graceful. I met her in the North of Ireland and liked her right away. I think you would admire her too."

"What is she—an Irish coed?"

"She's an American heiress."

"You've said that sort of thing before, and it doesn't always bear out. Is she beautiful, poised, clever, quiet, and rich? Otherwise I'm not interested. Rome is full of dingy people; I don't need to meet more of them."

"Libby Archer isn't dingy; she's as bright as the morning star. And she fits your description to a T."

Osmond waggled his hand. "Loosely speaking, you mean."

"No, I mean exactly. She is in fact beautiful, poised, clever, virtuous, and rich. And she's just inherited a tidy fortune, free and clear. I know it for a fact."

Osmond ran one hand through his grizzled hair. "What do you want me to do with her?" he asked.

Clara Merle shrugged one shoulder. "I don't know. I'd like to bring her into your orbit."

"Isn't she meant for something finer than that?"

"I have no idea what people are meant for," said Madame Merle. "That's for higher minds to discover. I only know what I can do with them."

"I'm starting to pity this young lady," he said.

She stood and he rose to his feet as well. "If that means you're starting to take an interest, I am glad to hear it."

The two stood face-to-face; then Madame Merle adjusted the neckline of her blue dress.

"Won't you take your flowers with you?" he asked.

"No," she said. "I have places to go, and I don't like carrying flowers in the street. It looks so common."

"You never look common," he said. "And you look especially fetching today. Your color is high. Like a Perugino Madonna. You never look as enchanting as when you're hatching an idea. You should promote them just to enhance your looks."

"I wish you had a heart," she said. "It has always worked against you in the past, and it will work against you now."

"I'm more sentimental than you think," he said. "It's very touching, what you are trying to do for me. I feel it more than you think." He reached one hand out and stroked her hair, as if he were stroking the flank of a horse. She stood very still under his touch, looking at him with her large eyes. If someone had just walked into the room that moment, they might have thought she was afraid. "But I don't see why I should give a damn about this niece when, really when . . ."

"When you've never cared about me?"

"When I've known a woman like you."

She moved as if to go up the stairs, and then stopped. "I won't make Viola say goodbye. She doesn't like me. But I think she's had enough of the convent."

"I will take your opinion under consideration," he said.

"I hope so. As to this other matter," said Madame Merle, over her shoulder. "Do your best."

"My best to what?" asked Osmond.

"Why, to marry her, of course." Then she was gone.

Chapter Twelve

It was the height of June before Madame Merle arranged for Libby and Gilbert Osmond to meet. She had given the matter her deepest consideration. Madame Merle was nothing if not deep. She knew that Mrs. Sachs was impressed by Osmond and his exquisite manners, so it would have been an easy matter to wrangle him an invitation to her house. Or there were any number of concerts and gallery openings that season where the two might have been made to cross paths.

Libby was eager to meet people—the world was open to her, as her aunt had said. Madame Merle possessed a small income but a large circle of friends. Mrs. Sachs was glad to leave the socializing aspect of Libby's education to her friend. The older lady was feeling her age these days and tired more easily. She would not have said that she pined for her late husband, but she felt as if the center of things had dropped out. And she hadn't seen her son, Lazarus, in months—he stayed fastened to the Riviera, listening to his new transistor radio, from what she could tell, but making up one excuse after another about why he could not travel to Rome. She was worried and disappointed, and both of those emotions fatigued her.

Madame Merle was delicate and cautious in how much she said to her young friend about this man, Gilbert Osmond. She had already spoken of him, and she knew that Libby had a good memory for such things. She would not for the world appear to oversell the man; if anything she tried to underplay his charms.

"He can be shy and awkward around new people," she warned Libby. "He may not want to be 'met.' He's peculiar that way. He worries that people won't have a good time. He prepares and agonizes over every detail. And then they show up, and he acts like a wounded prince living in exile."

"He doesn't sound like anyone else in Rome," said Libby, her curiosity aroused. She suddenly hoped very much that she would be welcomed by this shy, hermetic character.

"Gilbert Osmond isn't like anyone you've met anywhere in the whole world," answered Madame Merle gaily. "Well, let me see what I can do to inspire an invitation."

Libby was therefore gratified and surprised when, some few days later, she received an invitation to Gilbert Osmond's villa on the Palatine Hill. The note was written on a creamy paper bordered in a deep purplish-red color like the last drops of wine in a glass. Even the handwriting was distinctive—so beautifully formed that it seemed almost feminine, yet at the same time suggested a masculine hand. The message seemed to have been written in a fountain pen; the ink was very black. He had written, "I would be glad to meet—and for you to know my daughter, Viola."

Their appointment was for a Sunday afternoon, and Madame Merle assured Libby that it would be a very select gathering, just four of them: Gilbert Osmond; his lovely young daughter, Viola; Libby; and Madame Merle herself. But when they arrived, there was a fifth member added to the party, a sharp-faced, birdlike woman who sat at the very center of the room, her plumage glittering and scintillating from head to foot. She wore the kind of tight-fitting, form-revealing clothing that would not be popular for another decade, and heels so high and thin it seemed impossible at first that she could balance on them. Her voice was high and shrill. Her gestures were vulgar. Everything about her, Libby decided on the spot, was artificial and forced.

"This is my sister, the Countess Gemini," said Osmond, with a look of apology.

"But you must call me Amy!" the woman warbled so piercingly that Libby found herself doubting even the name.

"And this," said Osmond, with a good deal more pride, "is my daughter, Viola. She's been wanting to show you her drawings. She understands you are a lover of art." His voice, perhaps especially in contrast to his sister's, was soothing, like the sound of a cello, with hints of richer tones beneath and just the faintest trace of an Italian accent.

"I do love art, but I am not a judge," said Libby quietly, shaking the little girl's shy hand. She thought she saw relief in the girl's face.

"I adore art, and I *am* a judge!" screamed the Countess Gemini. "Let's see if the child has any aptitude!"

"Perhaps later," said Madame Merle, stepping between the Countess and Libby. As Viola led her guest dutifully toward some drawings and watercolor sketches laid out at the far end of the room, taking Libby trustingly by the hand, Madame Merle said through clenched teeth, "What on earth is she doing here?"

"I could hardly throw her out," said Osmond, just as quietly.

"What are you two whispering about?" demanded the Countess. "You're always plotting and scheming behind my back."

Libby and Viola, meanwhile, stood at the far end of the room looking together at the girl's work. "You have a very sure hand," said Libby.

"I always try my best," said the girl.

"And this kitten"—Libby pointed—"looks very sweet."

"Oh yes, she is adorable!" exclaimed Viola. "She has the most beautiful big gray eyes, you can't imagine. She used to sometimes come and curl at the foot of my bed at the convent. I miss her dreadfully! Her name is Mimi, which is the perfect name for her."

Though Libby could not have known it, this amounted to a very long speech from Viola. Apparently Libby had hit upon a favorite topic when she praised the kitten. She gave a sympathetic smile.

"I too had a cat that I loved," said Libby.

"If she's dead, please don't tell me," said Viola. "I can't bear sad stories—especially about animals."

"Do you care for art very much?" asked Libby, smoothly changing the subject.

Viola's shyness returned. "I like to draw," said the girl. "But I will never be as clever at it as Papa." She gazed into her visitor's face, as if taking her measure, and then whispered with desperate courage, "I care very much for music! Very much indeed!"

"Do you?" asked Libby, smiling again.

"Yes, but don't tell the others. It's not approved of . . . entirely."

"Why not?"

"We sing religious songs at the convent. And practice scales. That is all." Viola shook her head sadly.

"I see."

"But I think that music is the voice of God," Viola said. "It expresses—everything. Even cats!"

"I couldn't agree more," said Libby. The two exchanged a look of sympathy just as Gilbert Osmond strolled up. He was pleasantly struck by something about the two figures standing gracefully together, like an ancient Roman frieze. He took his daughter's hand and held it tightly in his own.

"I'm so glad for you to meet Viola," he said. "I'm afraid it gets lonely here for her."

"Never with you!" objected Viola.

"I'll be glad to visit as often as you'll have me," said Libby.

"Will you really? That would be . . . a gift," said Osmond. "Do you hear that, Viola?"

"I do," said the girl, with a radiant smile. "I hope you'll come and see us often."

"I always keep my word," said Libby with a certain pride.

"We are delighted to hear it," said Osmond.

"Come back this way, over to me!" shouted the Countess Gemini, who had been moving cakes around on her plate without eating any of them. "I'm only here for the chance to see someone new. My brother hardly ever invites me, so I just invite myself. Sit down, park yourself," she beckoned, as Libby drew near, "but not on that rickety old chair. Gilbert has some good things, but also some horrors, I assure you!"

"I don't see anything that isn't perfectly lovely," said Libby honestly.

"That's because you aren't looking closely enough," said the Countess. "You may take my word for it! This chair looks safe enough. Pull it up, I won't bite."

"I have a few good things," said Gilbert, as if his sister hadn't spoken. "But not what I would have liked."

"You'd have liked a few choice things stolen from the Vatican—that's what you would have liked. Well, show her your old curtains and crosses if you have to, Gilbert, but get it over with!"

"I think I will save a tour for another day," said Gilbert softly.

"I would like that very much," said Libby.

The Countess glanced from one speaker to the other. "Tell me, my dear girl, aren't you ashamed of your country just now? Every decent man or woman is being tossed out into the street—writers, artists, actors. Next thing they'll be burning them at the stake!"

"Every country must protect itself from invidious forces," said Osmond. "Every person has that right as well," he added, with a look at his sister.

"Oh, don't talk to me about invidious forces!" cried the Countess. She snapped open a mirrored compact, ran her tongue over her teeth, and applied some bright-red lipstick. “Would you like to try it?” she asked Libby. “Something bold would look good on you.”

“No—thank you,” said Libby.

“I agree, Gilbert,” the Countess went on in a dramatic voice, tossing back her head and revealing a very white, thin throat. “There are invidious forces at work in America right now, working against the best interest of the country. They are creeping worms who set up their own committees and make their own rules. Senator McCarthy couldn’t do it alone any more than Hitler could have wiped out the gypsies single-handedly. One must have help, of course. And there never seems to be any shortage of that kind of help in the world!” The Countess’s voice broke. If Libby hadn’t known better, she might have thought real tears glittered on the woman’s false black eyelashes.

“My sister takes a drastic view of things, always,” said Osmond.

“I take the only view—the only possible view.”

Madame Merle rose gracefully to her feet. “Political conversations somehow always give me a headache,” she said. “I must be going soon. Amy, can I drop you off at home? It’s on my way.”

The Countess drooped visibly. “I talk too much,” she said to Libby. “I babble. Whatever is in my head, I say—but you mustn’t judge me harshly because of that. I have a heart of gold, really I do. Viola, come give your aunt a kiss. I have some of that chewing gum that people your age all adore—no, take it. Take it, I say! And you,” she turned back to Libby. “Here is my card. You must come by to see me soon. I run a salon, it’s very amusing. I think a mind reader is coming next week—either that or a medium, I forget which. Whoever it is, he will wear a turban, I’m sure of it, and he’ll tell your fortune if you like. I hear the queen of Persia consults with him. Wouldn’t you like that?”

“It sounds . . . interesting,” said Libby.

“Then you absolutely must come. Promise me you’ll come!” shrieked the Countess. She smiled artificially at Libby, revealing very sharp white teeth and studying her face. Suddenly she added, “And don't believe the beastly things that people say about me behind my back!"

"We really *must* be going," murmured Madame Merle. "Libby, will you come with us?"

"If you stay a little longer, I'll walk you around the beautiful garden, and then Papa will put you into a taxi," said Viola.

"That I would be glad to do," said the papa, smiling at Libby.

"In that case I will stay—just a little," said Libby. The garden did look enchanting through the half-open doors. The air inside the villa felt almost too soft, as if composed of dozens of cobwebs.

"I always miss all the real fun!" cried the Countess regretfully. Goodbyes were said and embraces exchanged. The Countess enfolded Viola in her arms till the girl gasped, her golden hair nearly eclipsed in a headlock.

Madame Merle had finally gotten the Countess settled into her car, when some instinct made her return. In the foyer, a glimpse of her host through the French doors made her catch her breath. Gilbert Osmond stood out in the sunlit garden with his arm around his daughter. Viola rested her fair head on his shoulder. He had never looked more appealing.

Had Clara Merle not known Osmond so well, she might have thought he'd created the charming tableau on purpose. But he hated to be on display. Any moment they might move and break the spell. Clara hurriedly set down her cat-eye sunglasses and found Libby browsing through a book of paintings.

"I've lost my sunglasses," said Madame Merle. "Will you help me look? Perhaps I left them in the foyer."

She watched Libby go, then turned to see that Gilbert and Viola still stood together in the mellow light of a Roman afternoon.

Libby too had seen father and daughter standing there. The girl's yellow head rested on her father's shoulder. She pressed tightly against him. They looked abandoned, Libby thought, lonely and woven together at the same time. Their life seemed, for an instant, so desolate. The scene caught at her heart. She could almost smell the sharp odor of juniper berries rising in the air. A spider's web swayed in the wind.

Out front, the Countess beeped the car horn impatiently, three times. Libby startled. She discovered Madame Merle's sunglasses lying on the hall table, retrieved them, and brought them back to her friend, who was apparently busy in her own search for her glasses.

Still the two figures out in the garden stood unmoving, entwined.

"They are unlike any other father and daughter I know," said Madame Merle.

"I agree," said Libby. "Let's leave them be."

Libby and Madame Merle stepped out to the car together, for the Countess had rolled down the car window now and was calling loudly in her sharp, coarse voice for all the neighborhood to hear.

Only when he heard his front door close again did Gilbert Osmond finally release his tight grip and murmur to his daughter, "You may go now." Viola had been holding absolutely still—her father so seldom embraced or even touched her. She had willed the moment to last as long as possible while he held her tightly around the waist, pinned to his side. Now she left him without a word.

Inside the Palatine villa, a breathing silence filled the rooms. Osmond found his guest again perusing the art books.

"My ears are still ringing," said Osmond.

Libby smiled but said nothing.

"I just remembered!" said Viola, entering the room. "I have another drawing of that kitten. Would you like to see it?"

"Of course," said Libby.

"I'll run up and get it," said Viola, tripping lightly away. When her golden head had disappeared from view, Osmond said, "You are very kind to my little girl."

"It's not just kindness," said Libby. "She's such an interesting little person."

"Is she?" asked Osmond. "And what did you think of my sister?"

Libby had the good grace to blush. She looked everywhere but at her host's face. And everywhere she looked, her eyes were met by some uniquely exquisite and perfect object. She had the sensation that once she left this house, she might never see its equal again, and for some reason that she herself didn't entirely understand, the idea of never returning to these rooms made her feel bereft. She began to understand what Madame Merle had meant when she described this man as living like a prince in exile. It was more remote than the most hidden cottage in a deep wood. "I didn't have time to form an opinion," she said.

"She's very unhappy," said Osmond. "She married badly. The man's a brute."

"I'm sorry," said Libby.

"I hope it doesn't seem as if I'm just making excuses," he said. "But one seldom meets a sympathetic character. I mean, *I* seldom do. I'd hate to think this might be your only impression of us . . . your only visit."

"I was thinking the same thing!" exclaimed Libby impulsively. "But of course I'll be back if you like. And you've no need to apologize."

"There are always reasons to apologize. I fear if I start I will never stop. So I simply don't start. But it would be a loss if you didn't return—especially for Viola. She has spent so much of her life alone, or nearly alone. She lost her mother at a very early age. We live so simply here. I can see that she's taken a liking to you. That's rare."

"I like her as well," said Libby. "I enjoy the company of young people."

"Yes, when they haven't been spoiled by the world," said Osmond. "It sounds trite to say so, but I do take it seriously—my daughter's preservation." He smiled sadly and fell silent. "I think I have lost the power of using words altogether."

"Not at all," said Libby. "Besides, I've been living a noisy life. I find the quiet restful."

Osmond came and stood a little closer. Yet there was something hesitant in his movement as well. As close as he stood, he kept a distance. "We live very quietly here," he said.

Viola, descending the staircase, saw the two figures standing side by side. She was carrying a drawing pad in one hand. She stopped on the stairs and took them in. Her face was glowing. "Papa has been so lonely," she declared. "I hope you two will become great friends!"

Chapter Thirteen

"I am here to see Mrs. Osmond," said the man, dressed in black from head to foot, handing out his card. Standing in the foyer of Osmond's villa, he looked like a funeral director, but the card he presented to the surly servingman declared him to be a *critico*, a critic writing for *Il Mondo dell'Arte*, the most prestigious and conservative art magazine of its day.

The pale woman who stepped forward to meet him was as different from the creature in Parisian pink as that young woman had been from the girl in Bermuda shorts in Rochester. One transformation had supplanted the next. In Paris, Libby Archer had carried a look of intense, impatient interest. Now, it was as if someone had come along and shut off the lights. Mrs. Elizabeth Osmond—for Gilbert did not approve of nicknames—seemed a new creature. She dressed exquisitely, yet the effect was a kind of erasure, like the frame of a painting without its substance.

"Welcome to our home," she said automatically.

"Dear lady, it is I who should welcome and congratulate you!" The critic looked past her shoulder to another guest. "Arturo, I didn't see you standing there. Have you read the latest parody on *Signora Sorridente*?"

The *critico* hurried to join a small circle of men dressed in black, one of them eccentrically and elaborately mustachioed. Gilbert Osmond stood among them, greeting his newest guest with a languid handshake. Beyond them, close to the fire—for it was late winter now in Rome—stood two perfumed women speaking quietly. Other guests were scattered in the remaining downstairs rooms—intellectual-looking young men, for the most part, who wolfed down the delicacies laid out for them, though only after first eyeing them with evident scorn. The Countess Gemini was present also, poised at a small table in a far corner of the room, observing everything. Her dress was less ostentatious than before, though no less form-fitting. She wore a red polka-dot silk scarf around her narrow throat.

Only Viola seemed unchanged, marooned on her accustomed small sofa in the middle of the room. Her dress was a trifle less girlish, her hair a little more brushed. Otherwise she was exactly as before. She sat stroking a gray and white cat, which she fed little tidbits from her plate whenever she could be sure no one was looking. Of all the guests in the house, she looked the most isolated—and the most content. Libby took her place beside her stepdaughter. She stroked the cat's forehead with two fingers. The cat purred. For the first time all afternoon, Libby smiled. "Is Mimi enjoying her snacks?" she asked.

"Don't tell Papa!" Viola pleaded. "He claims she's getting too fat."

In answer, Libby laid her finger on her own lips, silently promising secrecy.

The Countess Gemini swept over. "Can't I get you to eat a bite?" she asked Libby. There was unmistakable tenderness in her voice.

Libby shook her head. "No, nothing."

"I can make you up a very small plate," pleaded the Countess.

Libby shook her head again. "Thank you," she said.

"Let me see if I can tempt you," said the Countess, scurrying back to her table in the corner. She began placing items on a gold-rimmed plate: a bunch of purple grapes, a few crackers. She busied herself with the arrangements.

There was another knock at the door, and Libby rose automatically, straightening her dress, venturing a glance in her husband's direction. He was absorbed in conversation. He kept his back to his wife. Libby moved toward the door, but halfway there she gave out a cry of undisguised surprise and delight. "Lazarus!" She flew into her cousin's arms, practically knocking him over at the doorway.

Osmond looked over, then quickly away, moving so as to stand now with his back entirely to the door. A new expression crossed his smooth features. The Countess Gemini watched it all from her place at the corner table, but Libby was oblivious, for once, to the impression she made.

"Darling Lazarus!" she cried. She rocked him in her thin arms. "Dearest! Why didn't you tell me you were coming? I could have had the joy of waiting for you!"

"I didn't know myself till I set out," he said. "Of course I had to come."

"You look well," she said. "I don't think I've ever seen you with a suntan before."

"Ah yes," said Lazarus. "The Riviera works wonders." But he added nothing more. It came to her then that in fact he didn't look well at all. His mouth looked tired, and his skin appeared more yellow than tanned, the skin taut across his cheeks.

"It was beastly of me to elope," she said, not meeting his eyes. "And then we took the world's most extended honeymoon."

Lazarus kept looking around, drinking her in, smiling and dismayed, trying to force her to meet his gaze. Finally, he steadied her by holding her by the shoulders. "How are you?" he asked. "Really."

"I have seen the world," she said simply.

"I see," he said. "And is it to your liking?"

"Parts of it are," she said, looking away. "But I must introduce you properly to my husband." She took Lazarus by the hand and drew him to the circle of black-clad men surrounding Osmond. He seemed not to notice her draw near, so that she had to touch Osmond lightly on the arm more than once before he turned, feigning surprise.

"Look who's here!" she said, smiling her brightest.

There was no answering smile on her husband's face. "Ah yes—it's Elizabeth's Irish cousin," he drawled.

"You've met?" asked his wife.

"Long ago," said Lazarus. "At Madame Merle's apartments."

"That I don't remember," said Osmond. "But I never forget a face."

"That's unfortunate, for a face like mine," joked Lazarus. None of the men responded. Their conversation seemed merely to have paused for this interruption.

"You sent a handsome wedding gift," said Osmond. "Thank you."

"You're welcome," said Lazarus.

The conversation was clearly at an end. Osmond again angled his back deliberately, to face his friends, away from his wife and her cousin. Libby looked surprised, but only for the briefest instant. Her eyes widened. Then the veil dropped down again over her face; the light went back out. She looked across the room and met the piercing, friendly gaze of her sister-in-law, the Countess Gemini, who shrugged and made a comic face.

Libby pulled Lazarus away. "You must meet my sister-in-law," she said. "And Viola! My stepdaughter. You'll adore her."

"Anyone you adore I will love," said Lazarus, pressing his cousin's arm.

As they moved away Osmond said something in Italian, "*Gli piace il suo*," that made the other men snicker and look again.

"Bulicio?" asked the *critico*.

Libby felt rather than saw Lazarus flinch as she guided him away.

"And anyone you hate I will hate," he said.

"Oh, but I don't hate anyone," she said in a quiet voice. "It's too exhausting."

Her cousin was quickly settled with the Countess and Viola, and together they watched the new guests trickle in. Libby jumped up each time to greet the newcomers and guide them toward her husband or carefully away, as the individual case seemed to merit.

"Can't he greet anyone himself?" Lazarus asked her at last, unable to keep the irritation out of his voice.

"He prefers not to," said Libby.

"He prefers to be greeted," put in the Countess in her high, sharp voice, just a hint softer around Libby. "If one wishes to kiss his ring, that's all right too."

"I'm sure it is." Lazarus stretched his mouth as if to laugh, but his expression remained grim.

Lazarus carried on a lively conversation with the Countess Gemini, but he was busy taking in the whole salon with his clever, hazel eyes. Libby could feel him taking account of the studied arrangement of the room; its carefully chosen, exquisite furnishings; the hushed murmur of voices; his host firmly enclosed by his eternal circle of black-clad Italian men. Now and then one man would leave and another enter, but the substance, shape, and tone of the conversation never appeared to vary. The salon felt airless. It was all very muted, elegant, like the Bohemian ruby vases and framed etchings. Never once did Osmond address his wife, but not till Lazarus was there to witness all this had she felt her own exile so keenly.

At last her cousin's patience gave out—as it usually did, abruptly and all at once. He closed his eyes, then opened them and looked directly at Libby, though the Countess Gemini was in the middle of another one of her long stories. Nearly all of them featured herself in some catastrophe or another, though she inevitably ended her tales with shrieks of high-pitched laughter, tugging at the ends of her bleached hair.

"It's stifling here," Lazarus said to Libby. "I must have some air. Can we go out for a walk?"

Libby rose at once, her brow furrowed. She was no longer the bright, quick, young thing she had been in Rochester. An admirer might have thought her wiser, tireder—and perhaps more beautiful. "Of course. I'll get my coat." She fetched a pale cashmere car coat from a room behind the salon and shrugged it on. The pale-blue color did not really suit her. It tied around the waist like a loose-fitting robe. She looped a wool scarf around her cousin's neck and helped him into his jacket, against his protestations. "Nights in Rome can be bitter," she insisted.

When they reached the door, their host spoke, without turning around. "Don't be gone long." Osmond spoke quietly, but Libby flinched as if she'd been struck. She did not answer her husband, she only nodded, and opened and closed the front door quietly. The night air was indeed bitter, but its bitterness felt like a blessed relief after the stuffiness of the crowded villa.

The cousins walked in silence down the steep hill. Lazarus shuffled slightly ahead, sunk in thought, his hands jammed deep into his coat pockets. Finally, when the road leveled off at the bottom he turned and waited for her to catch up. "I never thought I'd see you like this," he said gravely.

"In Italy, on a winter's night?" she asked.

"I never thought you would marry beneath you."

"Because my husband has no title?" she demanded with a show of coldness. "And no fortune of his own?"

"Don't be a fool," Lazarus said harshly. "You could have married a pauper—I half expected it. You could have married a waiter and I wouldn't have blinked. I wouldn't have felt what I do now."

"Which is what, exactly?" She stood her ground, mirroring him, her own hands now shoved in her pockets.

"Disgust," he said.

"That's a nice thing to say!"

"I'm not trying to be nice. I'm trying to understand you . . . to understand this."

"Marriage is always something of a mystery," she said.

"This is not a marriage. I know what I saw back there. Good God. You could have made anything of yourself, and look what you've become! Worse than a servant . . . the lackey of a sterile dilettante."

"Be careful what you say," she warned him.

"It's not that I expected you to change the world, God knows. You may have expected that of yourself, but I'm not even sure it's a worthy aim—the world being what it is. But for yourself, Libby! My God . . . look at yourself."

"Lazarus," she said.

"To scrape and bow for such a man," he went on relentlessly. "I don't see how you stand it."

"If you feel that way about my husband, you'd better not stay."

"I don't intend to!" he said emphatically. "I've seen enough tonight to last a lifetime."

"Can't you be pleasant?" she begged. "It's been so long since I've laid eyes on you. Can't we try to just get along?"

"Can you?" he demanded. "And if you can—how do you do it? It was never like you to lie to yourself."

"I always try to get along," she said evenly.

"That sounds like a fine life!" he exclaimed. He had stopped walking but now he bolted ahead again, his long legs flashing in the darkness.

She strode after him, out of breath. "I'm sorry I'm not Madame Curie!" she exclaimed. "I'm sorry I'm not something famous and extraordinary and noble!"

"If you had only been yourself, that would have been noble enough for me," he said. "But to cater to the whims of that man . . . nothing about him is real. His house, his *collezioni*, his airs, his little goatee. I see it . . . I can't help but see it."

"Not everything," she said. "His teeth are his own."

"I'm surprised you can laugh at such an existence," he said.

"I'm surprised you can stop laughing," she replied.

"Some thoughts lie too deep for tears."

"I imagine you're quoting something," she said. "But I don't recognize it. I'm not as clever as you are. I'm not as clever as you think I am."

"You're a greater fool than I would have believed possible!"

"Lazarus, in the name of God," she said. "I must ask you to control yourself. You are speaking about the man I married."

"I notice you don't say 'the man I love.'"

"When have I ever said such things to you?"

"Never," Lazarus said bitterly. "I wish you had. I might understand you better now! If I thought you had married him out of love—or lust. But that's impossible. It's surely only, only . . ." He stopped himself.

"Only what?" she persisted.

"Only out of perversity," he said. "As if you're bound and determined to prove that the most unlovable things in the world are lovable."

"You do say the sweetest things," she said.

"I'm not trying to be sweet," he said.

"Then you are succeeding brilliantly." But she took his thin hand in hers, and that silenced him. She saw, with horror, that his eyes were filled with tears. "Please don't be sad," she said. "Lazarus, please."

He did not answer but silently pressed her hand in return.

"I am sad enough for both of us," she finally said. "There—now are you satisfied?"

"Satisfied?" he said, pulling away. "Why in God's name would I be satisfied? I've only wanted goodness for you and look what I've done."

"I have done this myself," she answered quietly.

He tried a different tack. "Come away," he said. "Come back to Northern Ireland with me. You'll always have a home there. Never mind about the money—leave it behind."

"I can't." She shook her head. "I have to try to make this work, don't you see?"

"No, I don't!" he said. "This is the twentieth century, it's 1956. People get divorces. They start over. They strike out on their own. Why can't you?"

"Because I can't," she said. "I can't. I can't fail at this too!"

"When have you ever failed before?" he demanded.

"When have I succeeded?" she returned. "What have I made of my life—of my splendid chances?"

"All the more reason not to throw your life away now," he said.

"It's still early," she said. "I haven't given this marriage a fair try. And it may sound ridiculously old-fashioned to you, but I made a promise. I made a solemn promise, before God, and I must try to keep it."

Lazarus shook his head. "I see I'm not going to change your mind," he said.

"And there is Viola," she added. "She is my daughter now. She needs a true family. I am her best chance at that."

"Perhaps," he said reluctantly, "one day you'll also have a family of your own."

Libby bit her lip. In the darkness, he did not see it. "Perhaps," she said.

They walked on in silence a few minutes. Libby held out her hand, almost fearfully. It hung for a moment between them and then he took it, and they walked on, his bare hand holding her gloved one.

"I will come to you in Ireland," she said. "It's better. I promise you I'll come," she added quickly. "But now—walk with me back to the villa. It's so cold. You're shivering."

"No," he said. "I won't go back. Tell your husband—well, anything you like. You can say I am unwell. That's true enough." He did look very ill at that moment. "Do they have no taxis in your infernal neighborhood?"

"Just around the corner," she said. "Would you like to sit here a moment and wait while I fetch one? I forget that you shouldn't be out like this. Look at you shivering. You're far too ill."

"It's bad when people forget how sick I am," said Lazarus, "but worse when they remember!"

They drew around the corner and Libby put up her gloved hand. A taxi put on its blinker and approached.

"Don't forget to come," said Lazarus. "And don't wait too long. Remember the story of Beauty and the Beast. . . . Beauty promised to return but stayed away too long. He was near death when she at last arrived. But there will be no final transformation for me. I won't turn into a prince—not even for you, Libby. I'll only be a dying animal."

The cab pulled up beside them. It flashed its lights twice and honked, with Roman impatience.

"You'll never be anything but angelic to me," she said, planting a kiss on Lazarus's hollow cheek, a kiss so tender it seemed in that instant as if all of his sick and weary journeying might have almost been worthwhile.

"I'm afraid it's very dull for you here," said the Countess Gemini in her shrill voice. She had been pacing up and down by the narrow, iron-caged windows of the villa for the last several minutes, peering out. "Roman winters are filthy. People hole up in their houses. It will be better, come spring."

"Are you waiting for your friend again?" asked Libby. Osmond was out. This was not unusual. He was often away. Viola was upstairs in her room, practicing her flute behind closed doors, since the noise disturbed her father. She was very careful not to disturb him. He was one of those rare men who actively disliked music.

"Lady Jacinta, yes," said the Countess with a certain something in her voice that made Libby look up from her needlework. She never would have believed she would end up practicing an art like needlework, but Osmond approved of the hobby, and it helped steady Libby's nerves to keep her hands busy. She hated inactivity.

"You're very close friends, aren't you?" said Libby.

"Very," said the Countess. "She is married as I am."

That odd phrasing kept Libby's mind absorbed for the next few minutes, and then the Countess spoke again. "Speaking of which, I'm afraid you'll be losing even my poor company soon. I am traveling south with my husband for a few months. The winters are hard on him—he has arthritis in his hands."

"You are traveling with . . ." Libby put down the needlework in amazement.

"My husband, yes," said the Countess Gemini. She stopped her pacing and perched on the arm of a very good seventeenth-century chair. Had Osmond seen it, he might have shot her on the spot.

"I've never met him," Libby said simply.

"Gilbert won't allow him to the house," said the Countess. "My husband is not a monster. You can't believe what you're told. He likes men, and I like women. That's all. I hope I haven't shocked you."

"I'm not so easily shocked," said Libby.

"Not any longer," said the Countess, a bit drily. "In any event, my husband won't hide what he is, and that offends my brother."

"Isn't he hiding—somewhat—in being married to you?" asked Libby.

"It allows us to survive in this world," said the Countess. "But I suppose you're right. . . . Some people wouldn't call it a marriage at all. But we are very good friends, at least. I've seen worse marriages than mine."

Libby colored.

"I didn't mean yours!" the Countess cried. "Oh, my dear girl, I hope you didn't think—"

"I don't think," said Libby. "I don't ever think." She resumed her needlework with redoubled concentration and force—so much so that she pricked her finger and cried out in pain.

"Are you bleeding?" asked the Countess.

Libby held up her forefinger. One drop of blood hung there suspended. The Countess rushed away to the sink, poured cold water onto a dish towel, and hurried back to minister to the wound.

"It's nothing," said Libby, laughing. "Thank you. You should have been a nurse."

"I should have been a mother. That would have made all the difference. We both should have been."

"I am a mother," said Libby. "I have Viola, remember."

"Thank God for that!" said the Countess. A taxi blared its horn outside the villa, twice, then a third time. "There she is, in a taxi. Oh, the Romans! Why didn't I choose another city? All right, all right, *va bene*. But I must say goodbye to Viola."

"I'll say your farewells," said Libby, as the taxi honked again. "Go—go and be happy!"

The Countess kissed her. There were tears in her eyes as she embraced her sister-in-law. "It's selfish of me," she said, "terribly selfish, but I'm very glad that you're here."

Then she banged out the door. Libby settled herself again on the sofa. Upstairs, Viola attempted the same difficult flute trill over and over. She was a naturally gifted musician; there was no question about that. And she loved music; there was no doubt about that, either. Libby picked up the needlepoint, looked at it, and then set it back down again. "Someone must be glad," she said to herself.

Chapter Fourteen

Winter in the Roman villa remained very dull. Osmond held his salons rarely—once a month, always at the same day and time, on a Thursday evening, and the guests seldom varied. Osmond had not a great tolerance for company and preferred a quiet house. Even when he was absent, Libby and Viola obeyed his wishes as much as possible, with the exception of Viola's music playing, in which she restricted herself more severely than her father could have done. One hour of practice a day, and not a moment more. That was how they had dealt with music in the convent, so Viola believed a single hour was still permissible. Yet sometimes Libby would find the girl in her room, silently holding the flute to her lips, her nimble fingers running over and over the keys. She was a quiet girl, and Libby had learned to tame her own impulse toward conversation. It so seldom led to anything good at home, with Osmond. As Libby sat in the chair by the fire, thinking of Ireland, finishing her third needlepoint pillow, she could hear the ticking of the clock. It was the only clock in the house, but a very good black marble timepiece from Dinant, a find that Osmond had made several years earlier.

When the soft knock came at the door, Libby startled. She rose to her feet at once. There was as much grace in her movements as ever, but more hesitation. Viola was painting watercolors in a corner of the room, trying to get the shape of a pear right.

Standing in the wintry Roman sunlight, swathed as if in gauzy shawls of a light floral perfume, appeared her old friend Madame Merle, on whom Libby had not laid eyes since her marriage. She had vaguely heard that Clara Merle was traveling abroad. Her friend's upswept hair caught the light in its shining web. She was smiling, and Libby felt she should have been delighted to see her again, that she should have rushed forward to embrace her visitor, but some instinct made her step back instead.

Madame Merle's face altered perceptibly. She smiled crookedly. "Have I come at a bad time?" she asked.

Behind her, Libby felt rather than saw Viola melt upstairs to her own room. While she tried to cover her own hesitation, the girl's bedroom door softly closed with a click. "Not at all," said Libby. But still she didn't offer her face to be kissed. Instead she put out her hand and shook Madame Merle's. "Let me take your things," she said. Madame Merle handed over her soft cashmere coat—it was much like Libby's own, but in black, and rather more fitted—and unwound a scarf from around her neck like a soft green serpent. Libby hung them from brass hooks underneath the stairs.

"I'm afraid my husband is not at home," she said.

Madame Merle raised her eyebrows. "At eleven in the morning?"

"He has many hobbies that absorb his interest," said Libby.

"He would not like to hear them called hobbies," observed Madame Merle.

"You know him better than I do," said Libby. "Would you care for some coffee or tea?"

"Hot tea," said her friend. "Cream, no sugar. I learned to drink tea in England, and the habit has stayed with me."

"I'll make it myself. It's our man's day off."

Clara Merle nodded.

Libby realized, with an unpleasant sense of shock, that Madame Merle was well aware that it was the servant's day off—that perhaps she had timed her visit for that very reason.

"I hear that you traveled the world on your honeymoon," said Madame Merle, as Libby busied herself with the kettle. "Greece and Turkey."

"You heard this," echoed Libby, wondering.

"Through the grapevine," amended Madame Merle.

"There is a grapevine about the details of my honeymoon?" asked Libby.

For the first time in their long acquaintance, Madame Merle appeared at a loss for words. "Of course, I looked in on Viola now and then while you were away," she said.

"That was kind of you," said Libby evenly. "But unnecessary. The Countess Gemini was here with her."

"I was unconvinced," said Clara Merle, "of the kind of supervision a woman like the Countess might provide."

"I wonder what kind of supervision you would approve," said Libby. The two women did not speak again till all the things for tea had been laid out, and the tea itself poured.

"Marriage has changed you," Madame Merle observed.

"Yes," said Libby.

"I wish you would tell me why," said Madame Merle.

"I wish I trusted you enough to do so," answered Libby.

"Your aunt is angry at me too. We've barely spoken since your marriage."

"Why would she be angry at you?" asked Libby. "It is I who have disappointed her."

Madame Merle shrugged. She stirred her tea with a spoon, set the spoon down with care, and sipped the tea. "Won't Viola come down to say hello?" she asked.

"She will if she wishes," said Libby.

"She was never willful before," remarked Madame Merle.

"I would not call her willful now," said Libby. "But perhaps she has changed a little too."

"Osmond must not like that!" Madame Merle exclaimed.

"You'll have to ask him yourself," answered Libby.

❧

Madame Merle had the opportunity that very afternoon, in a sunken garden in a corner of Rome—one of the many hidden gardens that Rome's citizens know—and that mere visitors will never uncover. It was not beautiful in February, but it was private and the couple had met there many times before. The empty garden commanded a view of one elegant curve of the Tiber River, like an arm thrown out in sleep.

Osmond stood gazing out at it when Clara Merle came strolling up behind him.

"I thought I might find you here," she said.

"I knew you'd catch up with me eventually," he said, without turning. They stood shoulder to shoulder, looking at the view.

"You are disappointed," she said. It was not a question.

"Not in you," he said. "Never in you." But his voice lacked its customary timbre.

"But you aren't pleased," she said.

"Marriage isn't easy," he said. "It's not what I expected."

"It's still new," she said, laying one hand on his arm. He moved almost imperceptibly away.

"I don't think this will improve with age," he said. "She's very stubborn."

"I'm sorry," said Madame Merle, adjusting the green scarf at her throat. "I meant well."

"No doubt you did."

"Yet you say it as if you do doubt."

"No," said Osmond, taking her in at one glance. "I don't doubt."

"She was fresh and new—something I don't encounter often. I hadn't intended to use her," said Madame Merle. "I even thought, for once, I might make a simple friendship . . . just for a change."

"But we are not simple people," said Osmond. "And anyone and everyone may turn out to be useful—you know that."

"If I do know it," she protested, "that is because you taught me!"

He absorbed this in silence for several long seconds. Then, still gazing out at the curving arm of the Roman river, he added, almost casually, "I don't expect we'll be able to meet as often as we used to, you and I."

If she felt the flick of that lash, she hid it well. She grew, if anything, more erect. She touched the back of her hair with one hand, as if to assure herself that the hairspray was still holding it in place. "No," she said. "I expect to be very busy myself, in the future."

Upon his return home, Lazarus did not have to directly convey much to Lord Warburton about his cousin's new marriage to and life with Gilbert Osmond—if he said anything at all. The two friends had long since developed a way of speaking without words, a form of mind reading that both men would have laughed to scorn. The report might have been made in nothing more than Lazarus's selection of songs that day, played on his new record player, designed, as it happened, by Caspar Lockwood's company two years earlier, so that one record after another dropped down smoothly on the turntable. Lazarus had become an avid fan of Lockwood's various inventions and patents. Or the truth might have been told in his too-brief description of his cousin's Roman villa, or in a refusal to meet Warburton's eyes. Whatever it was, his friend's hackles were raised. Warburton felt a familiar prickling on the back of his neck, like a dog sensing danger.

As for Lord Warburton, his own motivations for going to Rome were unclear even to himself. He had a quiet sense that not all feelings need to be articulated—some are let well enough alone. When it came to matters concerning Mrs. Elizabeth Osmond—née Libby Archer—he knew better than to sound his own depths. The feelings were there—he had no question about that—but he let them lie as deep and still as they liked. He would not disturb them. He was a man of the world, a man of politics and business. He had lately begun investing in the stock market, something no Warburton had ever done before, and Rome was one of the major financial capitals of the world. He had every reason to go to Rome.

His sisters needed little convincing that he should go, because they already firmly believed that everything their elder brother did was right. The weather around Belfast that February was beastly. Surely it would be a little better in Italy. Their brother was susceptible to sore throats. He might avoid another bout of bronchitis if he went to Rome. He did not mention Mrs. Elizabeth Osmond to his sisters—there was no need. He might drop in on Mrs. Osmond or he might not encounter her at all.

Yet he found himself, the very first evening of his arrival, standing before the Osmond's formidable front door. It was formidable not only because it was barricaded with crossed iron bars, but because there was light and music within, which meant a party, and Warburton had not intended to walk uninvited into a party. With his uncanny luck and sense of timing, he had happened upon the one night in the month when there was a flurry of activity within the villa. He was ready to turn and run—in fact, he had already turned around—when two male guests swept up behind him and carried him inside by their own velocity. It was a bitter cold evening and they had no reason to stand loitering by the door.

Thus it was that Lord Warburton, that most proper of Englishmen, made his entrance uninvited and unannounced, flanked by two strange

Italian men wearing black. With his height and breadth, his fair hair, sparkling blue eyes, and camel's hair coat, he was set off as effectively as a gem against black velvet. Libby flew to the door with Viola trailing behind her like a beautiful pink ribbon. The young girl had mistaken her stepmother's cry for a sound of dismay, and though she wasn't sure how to help, she had instinctively come to her aid.

But now there followed a hearty shaking of hands and confused laughter; even Gilbert Osmond came gliding over, drawn by some magnetic quality in the new arrival. Osmond took in the whole visitor at a glance—from the top of his Homburg hat, which he now snatched off his head in horror, to the tips of his large, fine leather boots—and smiled genially. He placed one hand lightly on his daughter's shoulder, and with the other appeared to introduce the elegance of his rooms, and everything in them, as his own. "Welcome to Rome," said Osmond, as if he held the key to the city, the ancient empire itself.

Warburton nearly said that he had, of course, been to Rome several times before, but something made him hold his tongue. He thanked his host and bowed slightly from the waist, and the two men were soon speaking enthusiastically about collecting rare stamps. Libby hesitated, hovering quietly between them, ready to go, but a look from her husband told her to stay where she was, and she held onto Viola's elbow to keep the girl from fleeing. But Viola showed no instinct to leave. She was as fascinated by their guest as if he had arrived from the pages of one of her old storybooks. He looked as if he were—with his shining blond hair and bright-blue eyes, and the kindly smile he bent on everything he surveyed—not so much the prince in a story as a young king.

One of Viola's young admirers unfairly glared at Lord Warburton as he jammed a shabby hat onto his head. A magic circle had gathered around this unwelcome English giant. "*Buona notte.* I'm going now," he muttered to Viola.

She turned with a start. "Oh!" she said. Her blue eyes widened. "Isn't it early?" she asked. The college student would have relented on the spot—he was sorry he'd thrown his hat on in anger, now he'd have to find some way to take it back off—but Osmond broke in smoothly.

"It's late for boys like you," he said, and escorted the poor young man to the door so that he had no choice but to step outside into the cold. Madame Merle was poised at the doorstep, patting her hair, when the young man tumbled out.

"Buona notte!" she sang out. Madame Merle could have been a wonderful singer, if only she'd given it a try. She had dulcet tones and a true contralto voice.

"There's someone new here," the student told her moodily.

"Oh?" She arched her eyebrows.

"An Englishman. Lord Warbler or something."

The eyebrows rose slightly further. "Lord Warburton?" she said, in some surprise. The side of her mouth twitched in an amused smile. "Fancy that," she said.

"I need your help," said the young man.

"My help?" said Madame Merle. "Who are you?"

"I'm desperately in love with Viola," he said.

The smile threatened to turn into a sneer, but held. "Then you are beyond my help," she said.

"We are completely simpatico in everything. She could make me very happy."

"And you could make her poor," Madame Merle observed, "unless you have a fortune tucked away somewhere."

"Poor but happy," said the student.

"Why are you telling this to me?" said Madame Merle. "And by the way, it's brutal out here. Haven't you ever heard that you're not supposed to keep a woman standing out in the cold?"

"I can't go back in there," he said. "Not tonight. But you could put in a good word for me."

"What makes you think that Mr. Osmond would listen to whatever I might say?"

"He does listen to you," said the observant young man. "You're the only person he pays any attention to at all."

"And why should I help you, even if I can?" she asked, as if she had not heard him.

"I just told you!" he said. "I thought we were friends."

She patted him lightly on the shoulder, but it felt more like blows to the young man. "I have many friends," she said. "Don't count too much on my friendship."

"Then perhaps I can count on Mrs. Osmond's!" he said. "She, at least, has a heart!"

Now the smile did turn into a sneer. "Undoubtedly she does," said Madame Merle, in her velvety tones. "But do you think she'll do your cause more good, or harm?" And then she swept past him into the villa.

❧

The weather continued dreadful along the coast of Northern Ireland, with snowdrifts above the tops of boots. So Lord Warburton's sisters told him over the phone, though bad weather could be counted on till March each year. He extended his stay, and kept on extending it for weeks.

The Englishman became a frequent visitor at the Palatine villa. In his honor, though Gilbert never would have admitted it, the Osmonds increased their monthly salons to weekly events.

"They're jolly interesting, these at-homes of yours," Lord Warburton told his host, though privately he thought the word *jolly* exactly the wrong one. "I wish we had something like these at home."

"You see, my dear?" Osmond bowed slightly to his wife. "Soon the fame of your salons will have spread abroad. But surely you must have something like it?" he asked Warburton. "Some way of being sociable?"

"Yes," said Lord Warburton, tugging at the collar of his shirt. "We have dances and things."

"Dances," mused Osmond.

"I hope you'll come and visit Greyabbey," said Lord Warburton warmly. "Both of you. All three of you," he added, glancing over at Viola, who was offering trays of sweets to the other guests.

"Perhaps one day we'll have reason to go," said Osmond.

"You don't need a reason," answered Lord Warburton. "You'd be welcome any time."

"You are very kind," said Osmond. "But I always need a reason." Now he did turn to glance at his daughter, who was offering the tray to an elderly Italian couple sitting perfectly upright in a corner. "The wife is related to Machiavelli," said Osmond.

"That's just what I mean," said Lord Warburton, not looking directly at Libby. He seldom looked directly at her, but at any instant he could have told her mood, her posture, her dress, her slightest change of expression. He believed she had only grown more beautiful over time. "Jolly fascinating!"

Not long after this, Libby was alone with Viola in the early morning, braiding her long golden hair. That hair always reminded Libby of something, though she could never put her finger on what exactly. She supposed it may have been the gold hair of a princess in a fairy tale, some picture in a book she'd looked at long ago, even if it felt more familiar than that. Viola was holding Mimi in her lap, though the poor cat struggled to get away. Viola was always petting or holding the cat, as if she hoped she might turn it into a lapdog. They were in Viola's bedroom, the smallest room in the villa, but also the most private.

Suddenly Viola spoke. "I wish you wouldn't leave me alone with Lord Warburton," she said. The words burst from her lips as if she had been holding them in for a long time. "He frightens me."

"Frightens you?" exclaimed Libby, laughing. "But he's the kindest man in the world!"

"I know, but that doesn't help. He has the saddest eyes I've ever seen."

Libby stopped laughing. "Has Lord Warburton . . . said anything to you? Or done anything to worry you?"

"No, never."

Libby breathed a sigh of relief.

"He only looks at me. He's very kind, as you say. I don't know why he frightens me so much. I think it's because he is so much a stranger."

"Well, when you come to know him, he won't be such a stranger anymore," said Libby with a smile. She petted Viola's braided hair, and Viola petted and hugged the cat, who had resigned herself to her fate for the moment.

"That's the problem," said Viola, twirling around in her little pink and white chair. "I feel as if Lord Warburton must always be a stranger to me—always. No matter how long I knew him. And I don't need to know him any better than I already do . . . do I? In truth?"

The two exchanged a long look. Then Libby bent and kissed her stepdaughter. "No," she said. "You needn't do anything you don't want to do."

"Ah, if only that were true!" exclaimed Viola, burying her face in Mimi's silky fur.

"What must you do? You're not at the convent anymore. You don't have lessons."

"No, and I'm glad of it. I never knew how glad, till you came." She gave a little shudder. "It was very gloomy there. So quiet. It seemed the sun never shone inside those stone walls. I miss the music lessons, that's all."

"Well then," said Libby. She stepped back and surveyed the girl's golden braid critically. "It always comes out crooked when I do it," she said. "I have not enough patience."

"But I still must do certain things—even things that I want very much to do."

"Oh?" Libby undid the braid and began over again.

"I must always please my father," said Viola. "That is the most essential thing. I must not play my flute too much, nor ask for music lessons."

Libby did not answer this. Instead she said musingly, "Do I feel like a stranger to you also?"

"No," said Viola. "You seem like the most familiar person in the world to me. Around you I feel—well, almost as brave as you are!"

Libby's hands trembled in the girl's soft hair. "I wish I were as brave as you think me!" she exclaimed.

Chapter Fifteen

Soon, too soon, it seemed to Libby, her bravery was tested. Osmond sought her out one night, as he seldom did anymore. He needed her help, he explained, in identifying duplicates in his stamp collection. It was a very fine collection that he owned, of valuable, old stamps. Some differences were so subtle that it required an expert eye to tell the difference in coloration. For this purpose, he had laid out two magnifying glasses on his large ebony desk. Libby had already gone to bed, but she dutifully put on a robe and came downstairs to help. Viola had been asleep for hours. Osmond had laid out everything for this work of identification.

"In my early collecting days," Osmond told his wife, "I sometimes got carried away and bought the same thing twice. I've always had a contempt for collectors who have two of everything. One is sufficient. One is perfect."

"Yet you've had two wives," observed Libby.

"Not at the same time," said Osmond with a thin smile.

"You never do speak of her."

"There is so little to say. She died young." He handed Libby the smaller of the two magnifying glasses and gave her instructions on what to look for. "But as we are speaking of marriage, I should ask—what are Lord Warburton's intentions, do you think?"

"His . . . intentions?" asked Libby faintly, setting down the magnifying glass. At a glance from her husband, she picked it up again. "I'm sure he has no intentions in that direction."

"I hope you are wrong," said Osmond. "He was interested enough once to ask you to marry him."

"That was a long time ago," said Libby. "It's all in the past."

"For you of course. But I'm not speaking of you. He's still a young man, relatively speaking."

"Of whom are you speaking then?"

"Don't be a fool. I'm thinking of Viola."

Now Libby did lay down the magnifying glass, with a clatter that made her husband frown deeply. "Viola is a child!"

"She is sixteen. In ancient Rome, she'd be a matron by now, with a family of her own."

"We are not living in ancient Rome!" exclaimed Libby, her color high in her cheekbones. She had grown quite thin over the past several months.

"More's the pity," observed her husband. "I believe I would have preferred it."

"Yes, I think you would," she said.

"In any event, she could pass for eighteen," he went on. "If dressed properly."

"Are you saying we should lie to Lord Warburton?"

"Why must you always put things in the ugliest light?" he said. "Kindly look for the stamp with a small blue flower and a crown on top," he added. "I don't ask for your help very often. You could at least try."

She picked up the glass again with a look of resignation and devoted herself to studying the stamps laid out in albums in front of her. There were a great many designs, so many it made her head swim.

"I believe you still have influence over our visitor. I would take it as a great favor if you would encourage Lord Warburton, in regard to Viola."

"And if I can't . . . ?"

He looked at her directly. "I would look upon it as an act of the worst disloyalty. Things between us could get very ugly."

"Uglier than they are right now?"

"You have never seen me truly angry," he said.

"Are you trying to frighten me?" she said. "Here—here is your stamp." She pushed it across the table at him.

He looked at it, shook his head, and pushed it back with the tips of two fingers. "I said pale blue. You must pay attention. Patience. I'm not trying to frighten you, Elizabeth. I am encouraging you to be a positive helpmeet to me—for once. Just because he didn't suit you, we can't pretend that Warburton wouldn't make a very good husband for someone. He has every possible virtue."

"For someone—yes."

"Why not for Viola? I have high aspirations for my daughter. I see no reason why she shouldn't have a fortune of her own. Thanks to you, she's done with the convent now. She has nothing useful to do. They appear to get along, the two of them. I see nothing on earth to stand against it—unless for some reason of your own you are hoping to keep him single."

"Why would I hope to do that?" demanded Libby.

"Why indeed?" said Osmond. "Unless perhaps, on the off chance . . . it might be useful for you to keep him waiting in the wings."

She set down the magnifying glass, quietly this time, and put her head in her hands. "You do not know me at all," she said. "It's as if we'd never met. As if we'd never lived together as husband and wife."

"I am glad to be wrong," he said in a slightly mollified voice. "Then you *will* help?"

She looked at him. "What if—what if she prefers to wait?"

He laughed. "Who or what is she waiting for? Men like Warburton don't come along every day. Don't be a fool."

"She is still very young."

He shrugged. "Will you help me or not? That is the only question."

"I will see what I can do," she said wearily. "Here. This one is pale blue. With four petals." She slid it across the table, and he studied it closely for a moment.

"What will you do with it?" she asked.

"The spare?" He shrugged again. "It's not worth much. And of course, the more there are in circulation, the less valuable they become. It's a pretty little thing," he said, leaning a little closer. "But I suppose I will have to destroy it."

The Countess Gemini, returned from her travels abroad, attached herself at once to Lord Warburton. They made an extremely odd couple—she was so small and curvy and glittering and he so tall and square and plain. Yet they got along well. The Countess liked to provoke him, with her sharp jokes and barbs, and he seemed to relish being provoked. She took in everything with her sharp, dark eyes, like the eyes of some wild woodland animal perched on a Louis Quinze sofa. At that moment she was watching him pick up a pair of Libby's light-blue gloves. He touched them with one large forefinger, as tenderly as a big man could appear to do anything, and then he set them gently back down again.

"Your brother is very clever," he told her.

"Yes, he had a genius for upholstery." They looked at each other and smiled. "And what do you think of my niece?" asked the Countess Gemini. Viola was perched on a high stool not far away, dabbing a paintbrush into a bowl of water to clean it. Her painted pear now looked very much like a painted pear.

Lord Warburton set his cup of tea down in its saucer. "I think she is the dearest little maid in the world," he said.

"She's very young," answered the Countess.

"How old is she, exactly? No one will give me a straight answer."

"I mean for her age. She is young for her age."

"Well, whatever age she is, I think she is perfect."

"What do you like best about her?" asked the Countess bluntly.

"Best?" asked Lord Warburton.

"Yes," said the Countess. "I can see you do like her. But what do you like best about her?"

"What a funny question," said Lord Warburton.

"I don't think so," insisted the Countess. "I could easily tell you what I like best about people. There is a woman of my acquaintance, for instance, an Italian noblewoman—but I won't risk boring you with exquisite details. What I love best about my niece is very simple. I love her innocence. It is so rare and precious—even to someone as jaded as me. I'm not sure I was ever as good as Viola, even as a small child. Her heart is as pure as a pane of glass."

"But not as fragile, I hope," said Lord Warburton with a smile.

"I hope not as well. And of course, she is quite beautiful."

"But that's not what we like best about her," said her companion.

"And so?" The Countess measured out a glass of sherry for herself. She never drank tea if she could avoid it. It seemed to her a barbaric drink, like most things English.

"She is very sweet tempered."

"So she is, indeed," agreed the Countess. "She has been carefully trained for that."

"I think it is charming," said Lord Warburton staunchly, watching the young lady in question hesitate with her hand over the watercolor paper, brush in hand. She was pursing her lips in concentration, oblivious to everything else in the world.

"No doubt . . . but are you sure it's what you like best about her?"

"Is there some quality I am too dense to see?"

The Countess looked significantly at Libby's pair of pale-blue gloves lying on the table, the leather fingers touching almost in an attitude of prayer. "Are you sure it isn't her proximity to someone else?"

Lord Warburton flushed. His eyes looked very deep at that instant. "Good God!" he exclaimed. "What do you take me for?"

The Countess did not answer this. She took a sip of her sherry and eyed Lord Warburton over the rim of the glass. She said, "We can't help whom we love. But we can choose what to do about it. Whom we put at risk."

Warburton set the tea down on the small glass table beside him with a clatter. He spoke in a soft voice, but the tone was urgent. "Do you believe I am endangering her? If so, you must tell me at once."

The Countess touched his knee. "You are speaking of the stepmother. I am thinking of my niece. My brother is a very determined man. He does not think of his daughter as a child, but rather as . . . an asset. It is not wise to disappoint him. I speak from experience."

"I see," said Lord Warburton. He glanced around the room, as if seeing it for the first time. He looked at the fine china in which his tea had been served, the sweets and rolls, carefully purchased and laid out. He felt on his broad shoulders the early spring sunlight filtering faintly through the barred windows. "I will go home to Ireland tomorrow," he said.

"Be sure to send a note," she said. "And make a very good excuse. Osmond cares that the forms be observed."

"But he won't be happy no matter what I say."

She gave him a long piercing look. "No . . . he won't be happy. Thank God you are not responsible for my brother's happiness."

"But he will take it out on her."

"He may likely take it out on both of them, but it will pass. And now," she said, rising, "it really isn't wise for me to appear to have spent this much time talking to you. I am lucky that our hosts were out this morning."

"I suspect luck had little to do with it!" exclaimed Lord Warburton.

The black marble clock ticked audibly in the villa's parlor. Countess Gemini was absent; only Osmond, Viola, and Libby sat together. The things were laid out for a late afternoon tea, and had remained untouched. Now it was growing dark. There was an air of expectancy in the room; everyone in it was waiting for something. Finally it came—a muffled knock at the door, and a note was delivered. Libby opened it, read it, and laid it down without a word.

"He isn't coming tonight?" inquired Osmond. "Has your English friend taken ill?"

"He's been called back to Ireland on business," she said. "Something came up that required his attention."

"His attention," echoed Osmond, his lips compressed. "I wonder that he didn't phone, at least. This is the twentieth century."

"The British are very formal people."

"What else did he say?"

"You are welcome to read the note yourself." She handed the paper to her husband, who scanned it, twice, then tossed it down.

"He says very little. We deserved better." Looking at the small sofa where his daughter sat erect with a frightened look, her hands clasped in her lap, he said, "Viola, go upstairs."

She fled upstairs to her room and shut the door. When the door had closed, Osmond turned to his wife with a look of fury.

"So you warned him away," he said. "You defy me in everything."

"I do nothing of the kind," she answered. "Quite the opposite. I try to please you every way I can, in good conscience."

"In good conscience," he mocked. "In good conscience!"

"Yes," she said evenly. "I still do have one."

"So you admit that you sent him away—against my wishes! Against everything I desired. Against *me*."

"I admit nothing of the kind. I did nothing of the kind."

"Then why this sudden flight?" he asked. He snatched up the note again and waved it in her face. "*A business matter of some urgency.* He doesn't even bother to make a decent excuse! It's an embarrassment."

"If it is, the embarrassment should be mine. He is an old friend. Perhaps I bored him."

"It was your job to keep him entertained—not *too* entertained. That is all. And even that small task you couldn't manage."

"I'm sorry," she said with a helpless gesture.

"I am deeply disappointed," he said. "Bitterly. Do you understand? I hope he will return soon. I hope you will find some inducement to make him return."

"What inducement could I possibly find?" she asked.

He gathered up his things and prepared to go. "I leave it in your capable hands."

Chapter Sixteen

The next several days were very quiet, indeed somber, at the Osmond villa. The at-home salons had been canceled till further notice. The Countess Gemini still paid occasional calls, but she too observed the difference.

"If possible, your house is even deadlier than my own," she announced with a sigh.

"Don't feel obliged to come so often," Osmond said.

"Well, you needn't blame *me*," she said. "I have nothing to do with the sudden quiet of your life."

He was paring his fingernails with a short, sharp knife. "If I thought you had, I'd cut you out without another thought," he said.

⁂

Libby returned home from a visit into the city to discover Viola almost in a state of hysterics in her room. Her weeping sounded like the cries of a wild animal. Libby had never seen such an outpouring of emotion from the child; she would not have believed her capable of it. Libby felt her own heart stop inside her breast.

"What is it? What's happened?" she managed to choke out. Her mind went through the desperate possibilities, but Viola was sobbing too hard to answer. She could not catch her breath. This storm of emotion was so unlike the girl that it made her unrecognizable. Viola wailed and clutched a small silk pillow to her middle, rocking back and forth in a paroxysm of grief. "Mimi is gone!" was all she could say for several minutes.

Libby sat on the bed and put her arms around the girl. "Has she run off? Cats do that. We will find her, surely. I'll put up notices all over Rome."

Viola shook her head. The look she gave to Libby was full of despair. "Papa sent her away," she said. "On purpose. He said she was nothing—but a—loathsome nuisance."

There was no answer Libby could give to this. She stroked the girl's bright hair and kissed her face, and rocked her in her helpless arms.

⁂

That evening a very quiet trio sat downstairs together. Osmond read, licking his forefinger each time he turned a page. Libby plied her needlepoint, and Viola sat very still. Now and again, in an automatic gesture, she stroked the fabric of the sofa beside her. The clock ticked audibly, and every creak and noise in the old villa seemed magnified.

At last Osmond put his finger in the pages of his book, and peered over his reading glasses at the two silent women. "Well, this is a pleasant change," he said. "We don't miss that awful music, do we, Viola?"

"No, Papa," said Viola in a high, dutiful voice.

"It gave me headaches. Another time, perhaps you'll play again. Something quieter. And that smelly little cat—you don't miss her much either, I presume."

"Not—not so very much." Here the voice quavered. A few seconds later, Viola excused herself and went up to her room.

Osmond went back to his reading. But Libby turned on him. "Why do you torture the girl?" she demanded.

"Don't be ridiculous," he said, without glancing up from his book. After a page or so, he rubbed his forehead, as if he had a headache. "It's not good for her to become too attached to anything," he said. Then he added, "When she is grown, and married, and has a home of her own, she can have as many musical instruments and cats as she likes. As many as her husband will abide."

A week passed. Then two. It was always just the three of them, sitting downstairs in silence for a few hours in the evenings. By day, they lived separate lives, but for this time each evening it was necessary to behave as if nothing had changed in the household. Osmond made it clear that he expected this. The radio played music in the background, very softly. This was Libby's doing. Soft as it was, it irritated Osmond and he threw it a glance of annoyance now and again as if it might turn itself off.

Viola had not been eating or sleeping well. Libby mentioned the fact to her husband, and proposed also, not for the first time, that he might consider allowing the girl to have flute lessons outside of the house, perhaps at a music conservatory.

"Stay out of this," Osmond warned his wife. "It has nothing to do with you."

"I disagree," said Libby. She had tried everything she could think of: flattery, reason, bargaining, silence, begging. None of it had worked, and each approach had to be carefully timed and paced to avoid raising his temper. Above all, that. For Osmond had one of those cold angers, which, once roused, never lost its capacity to feed on itself. Libby had seen enough to know that much. She had been walking on eggshells for days, guarding her every word and movement. She had dressed comme il faut and had changed her hairstyle to suit her husband's taste—he preferred the short Italian cut popular just then, though it didn't really flatter Libby's heart-shaped face. She changed to a paler lipstick and had her nails done. She trained herself to sit more quietly, to walk more softly, to keep his hours. All of this met with a kind of cool appraising notice, a nod, the way a passenger might look at a train that finally pulls into the station several minutes late.

"She is not your child, Elizabeth. She is mine. I know what's best for her."

"Undoubtedly," said Libby. "I was only suggesting—"

"I detest suggestions," said Osmond. "Especially regarding Viola. She must learn not to defy me."

"When has Viola ever defied you?" asked Libby.

"Resistance is a form of defiance," said Osmond. "And she won't stop crying. That irritates me. It makes me feel I am being accused. Am I cruel to her? Have I starved her? Beaten her? Thrown her out into the street?"

"Of course not," said Libby, trying to make her voice soothing.

But Osmond bristled. He stroked his chin. "I begin to think the two of you chased Lord Warburton away. Deliberately and maliciously."

"We did nothing of the kind. He has a mind of his own."

"Have you heard from him?" Osmond's head came up suddenly, snakelike.

"Only the note I showed you two weeks ago."

"That was nothing." Osmond let his head and hand fall.

"I was thinking," Libby ventured after a long silence. "Of a trip. For me and Viola. Perhaps to Paris, to buy some spring clothing. It might do her some good."

Osmond considered this, his light-hazel eyes on his wife. Then he shook his head regretfully. "No," he said. "I don't trust you."

"That is an unkind thing to say," said Libby.

"The truth is sometimes unkind. Besides, I prefer you both here beside me. And I see no reason to reward her for her petulance. A journey would be ill timed. She must come around on her own." He allowed himself a small smile. "Hasn't she read any of the current articles? A woman must smile and show a cheerful disposition if she is ever to find a proper mate. There's some truth in that, however fatuous the source."

"It's hard to smile when your heart is broken. When everything you care for has been taken away."

"Her heart has no right to be broken!" he exclaimed, casting his newspaper aside. "What has she lost? A flute and a cat! I am not above sending her back to the convent. Another year in confinement might do her good."

"For the love of God," pleaded Libby. "Don't send her away."

"I only say it could come to that."

"Please, Osmond."

He retrieved the newspaper and bent his grizzled head over it. It seemed to her he had gone grayer of late. She could almost pity him—almost. "Then drop it," he said. "Tread lightly, Elizabeth."

❧

"You must be patient," Libby told Viola upstairs in the girl's room. "And be prepared to be brave. I will do all that I can, and more. Perhaps, at least, we can get you your flute lessons."

"I am not brave," said Viola tremulously. "But I can be as patient as you like. I still have the flute, in its case."

The two women sat a long time together then, in silence, just holding hands.

❧

Libby was asleep, dreaming of her old home in Rochester. She did not hear the telephone ring in Osmond's room. In her dream, a back wing of the house had fallen off and she and Henry were trying to glue it back on. A muffled knock at the door woke her from the dream.

"Phone," Osmond said in an irritated voice. He too had been awakened. "It's Ireland."

A few minutes later Libby came downstairs looking pale and drawn, wearing a robe purchased on her honeymoon. Osmond was sitting in his favorite chair, reading a history of Rome and drinking a cognac. He looked up and watched his wife come slowly down the stairs. She looked at that moment more beautiful than she had in many months, he thought, almost like a painting come to life. Almost as she had appeared when he first met her.

"My cousin is dying," she told her husband. Then she looked like her usual self again, only even more unhappy. It was a disappointment. Nearly everything about her was a disappointment to him.

"I never understand why people make these phone calls in the middle of the night," he said. "What is one expected to do at this hour?"

"I must go to him," she said simply. She sat with her hands in her lap.

He placed a bookmark carefully in the pages of his book and closed it with a sigh.

"I don't see why," he said. "If he is dying, let him get on with it. I don't see what good you can do. It's not as if you are a nurse."

"I need to go," she said, clasping and unclasping her hands. She felt the almost physical presence of a storm there in the room with them, over their heads.

"It would be very inconvenient for me. I'd rather you didn't."

"I am sorry for that," she said.

"Don't be."

"I must always be sorry when I upset you," she said.

"I didn't like it when he came here," said Osmond, "but I tolerated it. I won't tolerate your going and sitting by another man's bedside. It's indecent."

"He is my cousin. How can there be anything indecent in my going to him now, when he is dying?"

He picked up a newspaper and rattled it, unfolded it, but did not read it. His words, when he spoke, sounded like words he had gone over many times in his own mind. "I am your husband. When we married, we made a solemn promise to stand by one another. I take that promise seriously—apparently more seriously than you do."

"If I didn't take that promise seriously, do you honestly believe I would still be here today?" Libby's voice was low but intense.

"I don't know what you mean," he answered. "I'm simply asking you to behave as anyone would in a normal marriage."

"Our life together is not normal," she said.

"Your place is here, with me."

"Don't you understand? I have to go to my cousin Lazarus. I must and I will. "

"I forbid it," Osmond said flatly.

"I see." She stood. They locked gazes.

"At least we understand each other," he said.

"No. We do not understand each other," she said. "We never have. And we never will."

By the time Libby had booked a car to the airport, arrangements had also been made to send Viola back to the convent for an undefined period. Osmond wasted no time. No one could accuse him of lassitude. He had packed the girl's trunk himself. Libby was distraught, but Viola looked like a prisoner being sent to execution, her face small and frozen and white.

"Of course you must go," she whispered to Libby, holding tight to both her hands. Her father had locked himself into his study, once the packing was done.

"I will come for you," promised Libby.

Viola nodded.

"Prepare yourself for that," said Libby. "I hope you will come with me."

Viola's eyes were wide and frightened. The rest of her face didn't move. It was as pale as a marble statue.

"To go where?" she asked at last.

"Anywhere!" said Libby.

The next half hour passed with interminable slowness. Then suddenly, it seemed, the taxi driver was at the door, hoisting Libby's bag over his slender shoulder.

"I wish I had my cat," said Viola, her voice shaking. "And my music. But it's asking a great deal."

The door to Osmond's study opened. There was no more that the two women could say in his presence. He watched his wife take her coat from the closet and button it from throat to hem. He said nothing. Libby embraced Viola tearfully, but the girl kept her eyes closed, as if she could not bear to watch her stepmother leave.

"Be brave!" Libby whispered in her ear. "I will come for you soon!"

She could not tell if the movement she felt was Viola nodding or trembling with fear.

Chapter Seventeen

Night was falling fast, moving from inky blue toward black, as Libby's plane descended into Belfast. The checkered green squares of Ireland below were wrapped in a shining mist, but as soon as the wheels touched down Libby felt a sense of relief, as if she had come home to a place she had never before known was home. The comfortingly familiar Northern Irish accents of the men handling the luggage and checking her through; the wool tweed cap of the taxi driver who drove swiftly and surely over the looping roads into the Ards—all of it gave her the illusion of safety, at least till she pulled into the driveway of Gardencourt and knocked on the front door, shivering in the damp air.

Her aunt opened the door wordlessly, and wordlessly led her into the house. She walked before her niece up the stairs and gestured wearily at the guest room door.

"I'm glad you've come," she said. "But the doctors all say the same thing. It is a hopeless case." She spoke in a dry voice, devoid of emotion.

"I am grieved to hear it," said Libby.

"I know you are," her aunt said. She looked a decade older than she had the last time Libby had seen her—more than two years ago, before her marriage. Angry words had been exchanged then. But the old woman standing before her did not look angry, only pale and stooped.

Just then Lazarus rasped from down the hall, "Send her in, for God's sakes!"

And then her aunt did smile, if grimly. "Go ahead. You can do no harm."

The man who lay on the bed was recognizably her cousin, yet he had a look Libby had seen before, as if he did not lie alone in that room. There was already a grim presence beside him, and Libby recognized it as much by its smell and flavor as by its shadow. Lazarus rolled his head to the side to greet her with a wide smile and followed her entrance with his eyes. His lips seemed even thinner, his teeth more prominent. She kissed his cheek and sat on the bed beside him. She had combed out her hair on the plane; it was back to its natural looseness. Perhaps it was better suited to the 1940s than to nearly the end of the 1950s, but she was past caring for all that, and so was her cousin.

"I was afraid your husband would object to your coming," he said.

"He did," she said.

Lazarus nodded.

Libby sat in silence for a few moments, holding his hand between both of hers. "You were right about him, of course," she finally said. "In every way. I am sorry I ever lied to you."

"There's surprisingly little comfort in being right," he said. "The monster."

"No," she said. "He isn't a monster. He's simply a human being. Not an especially nice one. I chose badly."

"I'm not convinced you chose him at all," said Lazarus. "I blame myself."

Her eyes widened. "You? But you had nothing to do with it!"

Lazarus lifted his one free hand and let it fall. He gazed at it as if it were a foreign object.

"You were only ever kind and wise," she said. "You gave me my first beautiful place to come to. A place of independence."

"That place brought you nearer to this," said Lazarus. "That was neither kind nor wise."

"The strangest thing," Libby went on, in a low voice, "is that my husband never lied to me. He never deceived me or pretended to be anything other than what he was. I did all that myself. He told me he preferred his own company to that of boring and shabby people—and he does. He warned me he was fastidious. He never tried to hide his distaste of what I call the world. I wanted to believe it all meant something nobler than it did. All my cleverness didn't keep me from being a fool."

"I know about cleverness," said Lazarus.

"I've had two miscarriages. Both times they explained that the baby had no heartbeat. After the second time I needed surgery. So that's over as well."

"Oh, Libby. I am so sorry," said Lazarus.

"Don't be. At least—not for that. Osmond never said he wanted more children. He already has a daughter. He likes only one-of-a-kind things."

"Leave him," Lazarus said. "I'll will Gardencourt to you. Mother doesn't want it. You can live here, simply."

"It isn't so simple," said Libby. "I wish it were. But here I'm upsetting you. I'm supposed to be keeping you calm and happy so that you can get well."

"I'm past all that," said Lazarus. "All I can look forward to now is a slow, lingering death. You'd do me a favor to help me make a quick exit. But why can't you leave the man? There's every reason you should."

"Every reason but one," said Libby, unsmiling.

"And that is—?"

"My stepdaughter. I can't abandon her. I love her. And Osmond doesn't. He is incapable of that emotion. It's my job to protect her.

And I can only protect her as long as I remain married to him. So you see . . . it isn't simple at all."

"Bring her here," said Lazarus stubbornly.

"She wouldn't come."

"Why on earth not?"

"Well, she's locked away in a convent at the moment, for one thing. And she has been well trained all her life to be obedient. To be dutiful. It will take time to convince her."

"Locked away in a convent," said Lazarus, shaking his head. "How gothic. The poor kid."

"She is sweet to the core," said Libby.

"I could see that." Lazarus's face twisted.

"Are you in pain?" asked Libby.

"It's not fun," he said. "The fun's over. I may even need you to help me." His eyes fastened on hers.

"I will do anything," said Libby. "Whatever you need."

"What will you do—with yourself?" he asked.

"I've started a small charity," she said. "I have a little money of my own. Osmond doesn't know about the charity, he needn't know. I go into the city often. He thinks I'm going to museums. There's so much need. I wish I could do more." She helped her cousin to sit up and then rubbed gentle circles on his back. Slowly, gradually, she could feel his muscles relax a little, and he closed his eyes.

"We all wish that," he said.

"It's a relief," she admitted, "to be able to tell someone the truth. The truth at bottom. I feel as if I have been waiting for that, all my life."

"What about that other man, Caspar?" he said. "The stern American. The inventor. Do you know I've kept in touch with him?"

"Have you? How funny of you! I hear he's working on computers."

"I made a small investment in his company," said Lazarus. "I should have advised you to do the same. It's done very well."

"You often tried to be my guide. I didn't always listen."

He winced. "There's a bottle of pills in my bureau," he said. "Yellow tablets. Will you get me one, please? They help me sleep."

She did as he asked. He swallowed it without water, then added, "Some guide . . . Virgil. Leading you into hell."

"I'm not in hell, entirely," said Libby. "And in any event, you didn't lead me there. I got here on my own."

"One man loved the pilgrim soul in you," he said. He took another minute to catch his breath. "That inventor."

"He is long gone," said Libby gently.

"I doubt it," said Lazarus.

"No, I only wish—" she said, and stopped.

"Wish what?"

"I wish my husband didn't hate me," she whispered.

Lazarus leaned forward then and took her hands in his. He looked into her eyes, as if to memorize something, or as if there were something he wanted her to memorize. "Just remember," he said, "if you have been hated, you have also been loved. Deeply loved, Libby . . . loved like fire. Blood and bone."

She fell into his arms, allowing herself to weep relieving tears. "My brother!"

❧

There was only one person Osmond disliked even more than Lazarus, and that was Henrietta Capone. Henry flew into Ireland as if she had been waiting for the call, almost before Libby could remember making a request. Henrietta looked as gaunt, upright, and elegant as ever. The eternal Mr. Pye hovered in the background or discreetly took himself off elsewhere. He always had someplace useful to go, someone to see.

Henry was not as impatient as she had once been; Libby could feel that difference. When her friend sat with her now, she was able to stay seated; one long leg wasn't always jumping up and down, her feet weren't tapping on the floor, ready to dash off to the next thing. There was a new stillness and thoughtfulness in the way she looked at Libby.

"I am sorry," Henry said the second afternoon of her visit. "I can see things are bad for you. I wish you'd tell me how I can help."

"You help just by being here," said Libby. "I can't believe how quickly you came."

"Oh, that was nothing," said Henry. "Mr. Pye arranged all that. England is just across the sea. A hop across the pond." She smiled mischievously.

"What about you?" asked Libby. "How are you doing?"

"Well, I'm out of work. I've been fired," said Henry.

"Fired!" Libby exclaimed and sank back in her seat, amazed.

"I wrote about the blacklisted," said Henry, "and I refused to stop writing about them. You've heard about the House Un-American Activities Committee, I hope."

Libby nodded.

"Someday I hope everyone will know. There are dozens of heroes and heroines back home, standing up for what's right, and we're not to write about any of them. Do you know who I got fired over?"

Libby shook her head.

"Lucille Ball! Who would have believed it? The red-haired comedienne. I admire her tremendously. I'll tell you, despotism brings out the worst in people—and the best. I can't begin to tell you how ignorant I was about the world, before I came here. And the worst of it is, I thought I knew everything about it."

"What will you do now?" asked Libby.

Henry shrugged. "Mr. Pye has me writing for a few of the English papers. Socialist papers, mostly." She smiled wickedly. "My mother is in hiding, back home."

"I can imagine," said Libby.

Henry crossed one long leg over the other and sat forward. "Mr. Pye has asked me to marry him," she said.

"He has?" said Libby. She had the sense that the whole world had been turned upside down and shaken. Henry fired! Henry on the verge of marriage to a foreigner!

"I feel at home with him," Henry said simply. "I have since the day we met. And I can't imagine feeling at home anywhere else."

"Then that's clear," said Libby, smiling.

"Yes, that's clear," answered Henry.

"I'm so happy for you," said Libby. She crossed the room to kiss her friend, but Henry hung onto her friend's hand a moment longer, to keep her close.

"And what about you?" demanded Henry, looking up at her.

"What about me?"

"Yes. What am I to do about you, and your cousin? I'm here to help."

"I'm afraid my cousin is beyond your help," said Libby gently disengaging her hand. "And so am I."

"I don't believe that."

"You must believe me if you're to help at all," said Libby. "I have come to the end of many things."

"But I am an incurable optimist," answered Henry. "That's how I am most stubbornly American."

"Just stay here in Ireland till it's over," said Libby.

"Then will you come back to England with me?"

"I can't," said Libby. "There are things back home I must take care of first."

"Shall I go with you?" offered Henry.

"No. These I must do alone. It may end badly."

"I don't believe that, either."

"You know," said Libby, with a rare, radiant smile. "I find your disbelief very comforting."

❧

The embrace that the cousins shared when she wept in his arms turned out to be their last embrace. After that, Lazarus lay patiently in bed, each day growing thinner and quieter. He allowed Libby to offer him soup or pudding from a spoon. He accepted the glass she held near his lips, with the straw bent toward him. His sentences were like telegraphs. "Thanks . . . enough." "Rest now." "No fun. Sorry."

Libby had lost her fear of the sick. She wondered why she had ever been afraid. She knew now there were worse things than death. One afternoon Lazarus didn't speak the whole hour she visited, though he never took his burning eyes from her face. Then, as if he'd been storing up his strength, he rasped, "Pill bottle, top drawer." She went and fetched it for him. His eyes asked her to open it, so she did. His long hand closed around the pill bottle, and his eyes closed too, his lashes as long and beautiful as a girl's. He was quiet so long she thought he'd fallen asleep. But he forced himself to speak.

"Third drawer." Again she fetched a bottle and opened it. The flat yellow tablets inside were identical to the first. He held one open bottle loosely in each hand. Her eyes asked a question, but she said nothing. He smiled apologetically. When the nurse came into the room he made both bottles disappear momentarily—a return of his old magician's tricks.

"Are you uncomfortable?" she asked, after the nurse had gone. She could call the nurse back if need be. She was tempted to do so, and to disclose the secret of the two pill bottles. But something made her hold her tongue.

"Will you have some soup?" she asked.

He grimaced and swallowed. His eyelids fluttered closed, then open, and his gaze was in that instant clear. He looked like himself again. His light hair fell over his forehead like snow. He studied her with his wide eyes. He leaned forward. "Adored," he said softly.

Libby woke in the middle of the night, coming awake all at once. She felt a presence in the room at the foot of her bed. She could make out her cousin's crooked outline. It did not occur to her to wonder how he had gotten the strength to drag himself out of bed and down the long hall to her room. She heard the soft, hoarse sound of his breathing, and even in the darkness, his familiar white-gold hair lit that corner of the room, so that she could have found her way by its shining. The figure sat there regarding her, his head cocked. Then he rose to his feet, sparkling, and disappeared like mist.

Libby threw on her robe and slippers and made her way down to her cousin's bedroom. The night nurse was just leaving, looking grave.

Her aunt sat beside her son, holding his thin hand without moving, without even looking up when Libby entered, as if she'd been struck blind.

When she spoke, her voice was dry and harsh. "Go," she said. "And thank God you have no son."

The funeral was small, but Lord Warburton attended with his sisters and his brother, the vicar, who looked dignified for the occasion and who conducted the service in Latin.

"It doesn't matter that we are Jewish," said her aunt Sachs. "At times like these, none of that matters. The nearest rabbi lives thirty miles off and never knew Lazarus."

About the manner of his dying, her aunt only said, "I don't know how he got the strength." Then, later, "I am not angry, you know. I'm only sorry he didn't ask me for the pills. I'd have done the same."

After the service, Libby found Lord Warburton alone, lingering for a moment in the corner of the drawing room. He seemed to want to say something, but she sensed his embarrassment.

"Thank you so much for everything," she said.

He regarded her with red-rimmed eyes.

"I understand congratulations are in order," she said, putting out her hand. She had heard about his engagement almost immediately upon her arrival, from the maid Margaret. She wasn't sure Margaret would ever forgive her for not marrying Lord Warburton.

"Yes," he answered with a sad, shy look. He gazed out over her head—but that was on account of his height. It was a habit with him, a way of hiding his expression. "It's odd, the way that life surprises you. I was so sure I could never."

"And I was so sure you could," she said. It was the first time either had smiled all day, and they felt the relief of it.

Then the large man wiped his eyes with the back of his hand. "I will miss him all my life," he said.

"So will I."

"I don't make friends easily," he confessed. "But when I do—well, it sticks."

"Yes," she said. "I remember."

"If you ever need anything at all, you may count upon me—and my future wife. Janet. I hope you know that too."

"I do," she said, and then both of Lord Warburton's sisters came rushing into the room to comfort Libby, one taking each side, with looks first of anxiety, then of relief, at their elder brother as well.

Libby and her aunt held shivah as if they had been Orthodox Jews. They sat on low boxes placed on the floor and covered the Gardencourt mirrors with black cloths. Aunt Sachs tore the lapel of her best black jacket, and she took out a pair of scissors and cut a jagged line in Libby's black blouse as well.

"It comes back from childhood," she said.

The house filled with their Irish neighbors, bearing puddings and cakes and urns of coffee and tea. Henry bustled around, making herself useful. By midafternoon, most of them had already come and gone, and her aunt excused herself with a headache, over which the friends and neighbors murmured sympathetically, offering to return with remedies the next day. It was late spring, and there was light glowing in the deep-blue sky. There was another knock on the door, and Margaret went to answer it, and stood with a stranger at her side, standing tall and erect, his hat in his hands. It was Caspar Lockwood.

He was at Libby's side in two quick strides. "I didn't think," he said. "I just came."

Libby could not speak. His appearance surprised her almost more than the airy spectral appearance of her late cousin. Yet she felt as if she had summoned him. Caspar stood there with his tobacco-Indian profile, the sharply cut nose, and his lips, unsmiling and yet sympathetic. She turned to Henry, who threw up her hands in self-defense.

"I didn't ask him to come!" she cried. Then she stepped forward and shook both his hands. "But I'm glad you are here," Henry added. "I'm not ashamed to say so."

Libby could not speak. She was thinking that no one in her life had ever looked straight into her the way that this man was doing, as if her life were one long hallway and he hurried down it, intent, never losing sight of her for an instant. That look of his did not pierce but encompassed her, like sunlight around a helpless object. She had never understood it, never appreciated it till she had known its absence—until it was too late to accept it. Tears sprang to her eyes, and she was the more ashamed because they were selfish tears.

He drew her into his arms and held her. "You are very unhappy," he said simply.

When they could decently excuse themselves from the others, they walked a little way onto the grounds of Gardencourt. It looked much as it had when Libby first arrived, with the vast green velvety lawn spread out as if encouraging her forward. But its two most beloved figures were gone, Lazarus and her uncle Sachs. She bowed her head. The soft air seemed to be holding her down. She could be forgiven for grieving, she thought. She could be forgiven, even, the black sin of despair, today.

"I can see why you loved this place," said Caspar, gazing around.

"It is very beautiful," she said. It surprised her how in his company her voice could still sound calm and clear.

"I can imagine being happy here," he said, clasping his hands behind his back and walking ahead. She had forgotten how broad his shoulders were, inside the black jacket he wore. How dark and straight his hair.

"Can you?" she asked. He looked so foreign in this lush Irish landscape.

"I can imagine being happy anywhere you love," he said. "Anywhere that you are."

"Come with me a moment," she said suddenly, decisively, as if she knew exactly where to lead him. But she did not. She walked in and out of the dappled shade of trees, and after a while she took his hand and held it as they walked farther. She thought they must come to the Lough eventually, but instead they walked deeper into the gray-green canopy of leafy trees. She dropped his hand at last and looked around her in confusion. The fuchsias had begun to blossom, pink and white, in patches by the woods.

Caspar stood looking at her again—that impossible, deep look. His face was rugged and kind. This was what she had sacrificed. This was what she had thought of no use! Perhaps if she said nothing at all. If she held still here, close to him, but allowed not a single sound, not even the sound of her breath. She would not speak what was in her to say. Then it would be permissible to stand in his presence. His hair was short and sleek, like an otter's. He always smelled clean, of nothing but soap and himself. She held absolutely still for another instant, drawing the last possible comfort from his nearness, from the simple fact of his existence. Then words leaped from her as if of their own accord.

"If I ask you to come to me . . . ," she began. "If, someday a long time from now, I call—"

"Yes," he said.

"But I haven't told . . ."

"It doesn't matter," he said.

She let herself look him full in the face. She knew that she was memorizing his features, strengthening herself for the long difficult journey ahead. Had she always loved him? she wondered. *How many lives must we ruin,* she thought, *before we stumble on the truth?*

"Your cousin told me, 'Do all you can for her; do everything she'll let you,'" he said. "Let me help you now. Come close to me. The world lies all before us—it's a vast place. I know something about that."

"The world is also very small," she said. After a moment she added, "People will say I've run from my husband to another man. They will say vicious things. And it would make life hard for my stepdaughter as well."

"What do we care for the bottomless stupidity of the world!" he exclaimed.

Her head was swimming; the trees themselves seemed to be swimming around her, in eerie gray-green shadow and dappled sunlight.

"You have always loved me," he said. "And I have never for an instant stopped loving you."

Instead of stepping back, she moved forward. She knew later that she was the one who first reached out for him. "Be mine. Be mine as I am yours!" she cried—as if she had thrown away all other words.

Then his arms went around her and his mouth, his hard, unsmiling mouth, came crushing down against hers in a kiss like white lightning.

It was a kiss that obliterated everything—it blotted out the sun and the landscape. His heart was pounding massively against hers—she feared for him, it was pounding so that her arms tightened around him to keep him safe. She too was held in the terrifying brightness of their embrace, in his muscles and sinews and bones, and his body seemed to encompass her for an instant, to surround her as if something had shattered, scalding both of them. But when darkness returned she was free. She ran from the spot, ran as she hadn't since she was a young girl in Rochester; and she didn't look behind her. She saw nothing. She felt her purse hanging from her arm and banging against her side and then she was back at Gardencourt where the other guests still gathered, and she stepped in white sunlight through the doors as if the gates of heaven had swung open. She had not known where to go, or which way to turn, but now she did. Now there was a path.

Chapter Eighteen

Libby flew back to Rome in early May, a May as sultry as the Augusts she remembered from her childhood. The heat was intense; it swallowed everything in its path.

She didn't see her husband; she didn't know where he went, and he had left no explanation for his absence. Wherever he had gone, he had taken the manservant with him. Viola was still away; nothing remained. The salons had all been canceled; Libby was alone. It seemed not just a foreign country but another world. She felt like a stranger in the villa, someone poised at the edge of a chair, waiting for the chance to move. The Italian legal system was intricate and contradictory, like a long spiral staircase that never reached a destination. Still she persisted. She must have definite answers, she declared, but she might as well have been talking to herself. The lawyers skillfully evaded her questions. No one ever came calling, except, once, the Countess Gemini.

"I'm surprised you're still here," said her sister-in-law. "I had hoped you would free yourself."

"I won't be in this place for long," responded Libby.

"I'm glad I got to say goodbye then," said the Countess. "And I'm sorry for your troubles."

"I've brought them all on myself," said Libby. "If I'm unhappy, it's no more than I deserved."

The Countess regarded her with her dark eyes. "Not quite all," she said. "Perhaps you blame yourself too much."

Libby did not answer. She crossed her arms over her thin chest, as if she felt a sudden chill. If only a breeze would blow! But there were no cooling breezes in Rome this time of year. You went out early in the morning, or late at night, when the air was almost bearable, and in between you sat and held still, waiting.

"Let me see if I can make this easier for you," said the Countess. "Madame Merle has gone to visit Viola at the convent, on some pretext of passing through. Oh yes," she added. "I keep my ear to the ground. I hear what the ants are saying to the grasses."

"Why should she go to Viola now?" asked Libby.

"Why indeed?" said the Countess. "I suppose she is pretending to console the girl. But she is only trying to reconcile her to her fate. To make sure she accepts it."

"She has no right to do that," said Libby.

"We agree, then. I love my niece. From the first time I laid eyes on her, after her birth . . . such a tiny, helpless thing, and my heart opened. I can't do anything to help her—but I love her all the same." The Countess turned her intense, clever gaze on Libby's face. Her eyes reminded Libby again of a squirrel's, or some other wild woodland creature—hard, quick, and bright. She seemed to be looking for some recognition in Libby's answering look, and failing to see it, she shrugged and tried again, making a wry face.

"Let me start again," she said. She fanned herself with a magazine. She looked at the covers, front and back. She hesitated an instant. "Listen to me, Libby. My brother's wife had no children."

Libby looked at her blankly. "What do you mean?"

"Just that," said the Countess, a touch maliciously. "My brother's wife had no children of her own. She died young. And childless."

Libby tried to absorb this. "Are you trying to tell me," asked Libby slowly, "that Viola is not Gilbert's daughter?"

"I wish!" laughed the Countess. "No, she is his to a T. To perfection. There is no doubt at all about that."

"But the mother—"

"Have you really never noticed?" asked the Countess. "You've never seen a resemblance to some other woman—perhaps in the eyes? Or the bright gold of the hair, especially?"

The woman's face and figure flashed into her mind as if it had been waiting silently all along, half-hidden by the lace of a shawl, tangled in shadow. And now, here it was. Nothing could be more obvious. "Madame Merle," Libby said softly.

"Monsieur Merle had passed away years earlier," said the Countess. "It would have been very inconvenient for Clara. Impossible to explain away. But Osmond's wife had recently died, and she was such a quiet little thing, no one knew the details. It was easy to say Viola was his. What would have brought shame to Clara Merle brought a kind of cachet to my brother. The noble widower, raising his lovely young daughter alone . . ."

Libby rose shakily to her feet. "I see." Her breath came very shallowly.

"There it is," said the Countess. "I've wanted to speak. I was afraid you would hate me. And Gilbert warned me. I knew I would be banished. But it doesn't really matter, does it?" She looked at her sister-in-law for a long time, and neither woman spoke.

"Thank you for telling me," murmured Libby at last.

The Countess rose to her feet as well. "I'm sorry. You've had a terrible shock, I see. I thought perhaps you suspected—"

"One would think. But I have been that stupid."

The Countess crossed to her sister-in-law. Her fingers were bony and covered with jeweled rings. "Anyone can be tricked. It is easy to be fooled, if others are determined to deceive you. Now will you free yourself at last?" asked the Countess. "Will you free yourself—and my niece?"

"Viola!" exclaimed Libby, like a drowning person catching sight of the lost shore. "I must go to her."

❧

In the end there was not much Libby needed to take. Not much belonged to her. She left her wedding rings in a dish by the door. She had the sense, at every hour of each day, that she was reeling on the face of the earth, and she had no clear plan, no idea of where to go once she left the convent with her stepdaughter. She could not imagine returning to Northern Ireland, absent of her uncle and cousin. She could not somehow picture Viola in Rochester. Nor could they spend their lives wandering up and down the wide world, running from Osmond. He would be sure to pursue them.

She saw no one but the Italian lawyers, who still gave no clear answers, or rather, whose answers changed every day; she spoke so seldom that her own voice felt unfamiliar when she stopped at the corner *osteria* to pay for a sandwich and a bottle of mineral water. She said a few hurried words to the women who worked at her charity in the center of the city—she wrote out a large check and then left, leaving the secretary clucking in sympathy and dismay. She would continue to send checks. But she had no intention of ever returning to Rome.

She rented a car, a convertible. It had been years since she'd driven herself anywhere. She had in the car a small advertisement she had torn from the local paper, and she stopped only for that one errand, in the beach town of Ostia. Once back on the road, the ruins of Ostia lay spread out before her in alternating white sunshine and avocado-colored shadows. She had no idea that such a place even existed, so close to Rome. Everyone knew the Coliseum, of course, but these Ostia ruins were nearly as vast, and just as ancient, with crumbling stairs leading to nowhere.

There was a cardboard box on the passenger side of the car, near her feet, and inside the box, a small blanket. In the trunk of the convertible sat two suitcases filled with Viola's favorite items of clothing, in all the gayest colors; also her drawing things. She carried Viola's music and her silver flute in its black case. Libby drove through mountains, and when she came to the border guard in France, she showed her passport.

She stopped for the night in a small hotel near the convent. The cardboard box sat on the rug near the bed. She simply lay in the dark drifting further away from sleep, sometimes with her eyes closed and sometimes with her eyes open. Each time she turned her head she encountered her own face reflected in the hotel window. She looked younger and stranger to herself, as if she had returned to childhood. Her eyes, in particular, appeared to be wide and burning against the landscape framed in darkness. She waited for the white morning to come, for the first sunlight to burn off the mists of dawn. She half expected the ghost of Lazarus to appear to her again, but he did not.

The pupils had not yet breakfasted when she arrived at the convent so she was asked to wait in a large, chilly parlor while they had finished their meal. One of the sisters took the cardboard box from Libby's arms and, exclaiming over it, stored it for her in another room. Then the Mother Superior bustled in.

"Your visit will do her good," said Mother Catherine. "She speaks of you often." The nun led Libby toward the parlor, down a sequence of long white halls. All of them were bare and clean; but so, thought Libby, are the great prisons.

Mother Catherine gestured toward the parlor door. Something in her expression held Libby where she stood. "It is not good for the girl to be locked away from the world," the nun said. "We do everything we can to make her comfortable, but still . . . she waits, every day, for a letter from her father." Libby waited for more. The woman's arms were crossed, her hands hidden inside her sleeves. She nodded as if in agreement to something Libby had not said. Then she reached forward and turned the handle of the doorknob on the parlor. "You are not her only visitor," Mother Catherine said, and practically pushed Libby through the door.

Inside, the parlor was furnished with brand-new furniture that appeared to be old; with wax flowers under glass domes and a series of religious engravings hung on the walls. The room was dominated by a large wooden crucifix. But that was not what claimed Libby's attention. At the far end of the room sat a familiar figure, swinging one high-heeled shoe. Libby had known they might meet, yet she was not prepared for the shock of the encounter. It took her breath away. Madame Merle rose smoothly to her feet, but Libby made a gesture that caused her to sink back down. Something else in Libby's expression made the other woman go pale to the roots of her hair. Her crooked mouth quivered.

"I was on my way back to Paris," Madame Merle said. Her voice sounded high and artificial. "Viola is looking well. I like the way they dress the girls here. It's very elegant and simple. Of course," she added, "I am only here for a short visit, to provide a little distraction."

"I should think you'd wish to provide more than that," said Libby.

The two women looked at each other. Everything was said in that silence.

Madame Merle bowed her head. "I was sorry about Lazarus," she went on. "I should have sent you a card, or a note."

Libby said nothing.

"He did you a great service—I wonder if you ever knew how great."

"He was my friend," said Libby.

"Yes, but one service was above even that. I wonder that you never guessed. Your cousin made you a wealthy woman."

"My uncle did that," protested Libby, looking away. She found herself gazing at the large wooden crucifix on the wall.

"It was your uncle's money but your cousin's idea. Ah, the sum was large! Very large indeed. It gave you that extra luster that made you a brilliant match. At bottom, Lazarus was your benefactor. Think of that! You see, you owe it all to him."

Libby said, "I believe it is you I had to thank."

Madame Merle flushed. She said, "I know you are unhappy. But I am more miserable still."

"I believe you," said Libby. After a moment she added, "I would like never to see you again."

"I will go away," said Clara Merle. "It's time. Perhaps to South Africa."

"That should be almost far enough." Libby crossed the room, opened the door, and stepped out into the fresh air.

Libby found the young nun and took what she needed from the cardboard box she had brought with her all the way from Italy. It made all the nuns smile, the sight of her carrying the box's occupant. She was not above bribery. It didn't matter. She could wait. She would be cunning, and attentive. She would do whatever was required. Holding a flute case in one arm, and cradling the beautiful, tiny tortoiseshell kitten in the other, Libby stood outside Viola's door and waited to be admitted. She had within her now at last the key to patience.

Author's Note

This novel is an homage to one of my favorite books: Henry James's classic *Portrait of a Lady*, brought from the nineteenth century forward, with various changes, into the mid-twentieth. Many of my book's bright spots owe a debt to the master; its flaws are all my own.

About the Author

The author of more than thirty books for adults and young readers, Liz Rosenberg has published three bestselling novels, including *The Laws of Gravity* and *The Moonlight Palace*. She has also written five books of poems, among them 2008's *Demon Love*, nominated for a Pulitzer Prize, and *After Great Grief*, forthcoming from the Provincetown Arts Press. Her poems have been heard on NPR's *A Prairie Home Companion*. Rosenberg's books for young readers have won numerous awards and honors and have been featured on the PBS television show *Reading Rainbow*. A former Fulbright Fellowship recipient, Rosenberg teaches English at the State University of New York at Binghamton, where she earned the Chancellor's Award for Excellence in Teaching. She lives in Binghamton with her daughter, Lily, and a shih tzu named Sophie. Although she has homes in New York and North Chatham, Massachusetts, her heart is still in Ireland.